Water Fight

Ben crouched down and leaped at Jonathan, who stepped deftly aside and let Ben do a belly-flop. The splash caught Jonathan, but it also drenched Bart, who hadn't even been involved in the game. As if on signal, everyone was splashing water at everyone else, laughing like hyenas all the while.

When Jonathan finally escaped, Ben turned around quickly, sending himself and Pamela tumbling into the waves. Practically choking she was laughing so hard, she reached for Ben's outstretched hand and let him pull her to her feet until she was wrapped in his arms. The feel of his hands resting so lightly on her back raised goose-bumps on her arms, and she could feel her heart pounding. How natural it felt to stand so close to someone this way. To someone . . . someone who *wasn't* Matt Jacobs.

Books from Scholastic
in the **Couples** series:

#1 *Change of Hearts*
#2 *Fire and Ice*
#3 *Alone, Together*
#4 *Made for Each Other*
#5 *Moving Too Fast*
#6 *Crazy Love*
#7 *Sworn Enemies*
#8 *Making Promises*
#9 *Broken Hearts*
#10 *Secrets*
#11 *More Than Friends*
#12 *Bad Love*
#13 *Changing Partners*
#14 *Picture Perfect*
#15 *Coming on Strong*
#16 *Sweethearts*
#17 *Dance with Me*
#18 *Kiss and Run*
#19 *Show Some Emotion*
#20 *No Contest*
#21 *Teacher's Pet*
#22 *Slow Dancing*
#23 *Bye Bye Love*

Couples Special Editions

Summer Heat!
Be Mine!
Beach Party!

Coming soon . . .

#24 *Something New*

BEACH PARTY!

by M.E. Cooper

SCHOLASTIC INC.
New York Toronto London Auckland Sydney

Scholastic Books are available at special discounts for quantity purchases for use as premiums, promotional items, retail sales through specialty market outlets, etc. For details contact: Special Sales Manager, Scholastic Inc., 730 Broadway, New York, NY 10003.

ISBN 0-590-40793-7

12 11 10 9 8 7 6 5 4 3 2 1 7 8 9/8 0 1 2/9

Printed in the U.S.A. 01

First Scholastic printing, July 1987

Chapter 1

Pamela Green rolled onto her side and pulled the sheet closer around her shoulders, trying to stop her slow but steady drift upward out of sleep. She knew it couldn't possibly be time to get up yet, but the harder she fought to stay asleep, the more alert she became. Wasn't there some reason for her to wake up early, something important she had to do?

Suddenly she remembered. Her English final was that morning and she wasn't anywhere *near* ready for it! Unless she got up right now and studied like mad, she was going to fail for sure! Heart racing, she threw back the sheet, sat up, and swung her legs over the side of the bed. Then she stopped, dizzy and confused. There was no English final today. She had already taken all of her finals. She even remembered some of the questions. She had been dreaming, that was all. School was over. It had let out for the summer three days before.

She relaxed a little, even smiled at her own anxiety, but the feeling that today was important stayed with her. Then she remembered. On Monday she would be starting her job at the day camp, and today was orientation day for the counselors. That must have been what was on her mind. But it couldn't possibly be time to go yet.

She rubbed her eyes and pushed a strand of blonde hair off her forehead. The room was still dark, but the window made a rectangle of a lighter shade of gray on the far wall. Even as she looked, it seemed to brighten a little. What on earth time was it? The clock on the lamp table next to the bed said 4:48, but it couldn't be. She never woke up that early, not even when she *did* have to study for a final!

She flopped back down, rolled onto her stomach, clutched the pillow around her head, and closed her eyes to wait for sleep to return. It didn't. Whether she kept her eyes closed or open, her mind was racing along at a full, wide-awake pace. She tried thinking soothing, drowsy thoughts, but then she caught herself alertly watching for the first sign that the drowsy thoughts were doing any good.

With an exasperated sigh, she pushed the pillow aside and sat up again. By now the window was letting in enough light for her to see the details of her room, though everything was still in shades of gray that held only the slightest hint of color.

A slight breeze from the window carried with it a faint scent of flowers from the neighbor's garden. She could hear a few songbirds just beginning to announce their presence, twittering and chirping as if this were the most glorious day they'd ever seen.

Pamela felt a little pang in her chest, as if her heart had skipped a beat. Suddenly, she felt an overwhelming desire to greet the dawn. She stood up and went quietly downstairs to the kitchen. The lock on the back door sounded as loud as a firecracker when she unbolted it, and she paused for a moment to see if she had disturbed her father or brother. Obviously not. The house was still utterly silent. She carefully opened the door just wide enough to slip through and stepped out into the yard.

The lawn was cold and dewy under her bare feet. Overhead the sky was a pale gray, as if overcast with clouds, but the east was tinted with pale blue and an even paler pink. She put her shoulders back and took a deep breath. The air felt cool and pure in her lungs, and she wanted to run and run until she was exhausted, then drop down onto the damp grass and dig her fingers deep into the earth.

Was Matt awake or asleep? She summoned his features to her mind and thought very hard about him. She didn't seriously believe in ESP, but she liked to think that love could be felt even across a distance. Would her thoughts make him dream of her? The idea made her smile, but it made her shiver, too. Or was it the chill that lingered in the morning air that made her shiver? Her short summer nightshirt was lightweight cotton, not really meant for wandering outdoors in the predawn hours.

Almost all the sky was blue now, and the first rays of the sun slanted across the yard and warmed Pamela's face. She tilted her head back and closed her eyes, taking slow, deep breaths and basking like a contented cat in a patch of sunlight. She felt unbelievably lighthearted and happy. It was going to be a beautiful day, and she had a feeling it was going to be a wonderful summer, too. After a last look at the sunrise, she went back into the house.

"Pamela?"

She huddled deeper into the blanket and willed the intrusion to disappear. "Leave me alone," she muttered in a low voice.

"Pamela!"

Her blanket was magically whisked away. Light pried through her tightly shut lids.

"*Pamela!* Wake up!"

She opened her eyes a crack and peered upward. Her father was standing over her. She opened her eyes wider. What on earth was she doing in the living room? She knew she had gone to bed in her own room the night before. Then she remembered her date with the sunrise and smiled.

"Good morning, sweetheart," her father said. "Didn't you tell me you had to catch a bus at eight?"

She jumped off the couch as if she had just been hit by a stream of cold water. "What time is it?" she demanded.

"Relax," he said, smiling. "It's only seven-thirty."

"*Only* seven-thirty," she cried. "I'll never make it! I'll miss the bus and lose the job and never live it down! Why did this have to happen to me — today of all days!"

"Calm down, sweetie. Why don't you run upstairs and get dressed, and I'll put some breakfast together. Between you and me, I promise we'll get you to your bus on time. Is it a deal?" He reached over and ruffled her hair, then disappeared into the kitchen.

Pamela stood by the couch for another moment, hoping the rest of the day didn't go this way. Then good sense took over, and she dashed up the stairs to her room to dress.

She and her father reached the corner just as the yellow school bus came around the curve. "Thanks, Dad," she said breathlessly. She reached up to kiss his cheek, then crammed the last of her piece of toast into her mouth.

"Have fun," he replied, brushing a crumb off her chin.

There were eight or nine other counselors scattered around the bus, and they all looked up as Pamela got on. Three girls who seemed to be friends acknowledged her with quick nods before going back to their conversation, and a big guy with a scuffed-up leather gym bag on the seat next to him smiled and picked up his paperback. She glanced at the cover as she walked past, expecting some macho adventure novel. To her surprise, she recognized *The Catcher in the Rye.* Maybe he had mistaken it for a book about baseball, she thought, then chided herself for being so prejudiced. Hadn't going out with Matt Jacobs taught her anything?

She was still in the aisle when the bus started with a lurch. She grabbed the back of a seat to save herself from falling, then swung into the nearest empty seat. A girl on the other side of the bus caught her eye and smiled. Pamela smiled back shyly. The girl looked slightly familiar, but she couldn't place her. How was she ever going to learn the names and faces of a whole new crop of people? And it wasn't just her fellow counselors, either, there were the campers as well.

An idea struck her. She pulled a sketchbook and felt-tip pen from her book bag and drew quick impressions of the girl across the aisle, the boy reading Salinger, and the trio of conversationalists near the front of the bus. She would label them as soon as she learned everyone's name.

"Hi," a voice said from just above her. She

instinctively closed the sketchbook before looking up. The boy standing beside her had light green eyes, dark curly hair, and a half-serious, half-smiling expression that lit up his very cute face.

"You're Pamela, right? A friend of Fiona's and Jonathan's?"

"That's right," she replied, returning his smile. Jonathan Preston was Matt's best friend, and since Pamela had started spending time with Matt, she had become good friends with both Jonathan and his English girl friend, Fiona. "And I've seen you around the quad at Kennedy, haven't I? I think I even overheard you and Jonathan talking about some amazing new satellite you were designing. I thought you guys were plotting to take over the world, or at least the school."

The boy chuckled. "That's right," he said. "We're still working on it. I'm Ben. Ben Forrest." He put his hand out for her to shake, and as their fingers met, Pamela felt a flash of warmth shoot through her entire body. Suddenly overtaken by shyness, she quickly let her hand fall back into her lap.

Blushing, Ben said, "I'm a junior. I mean, I was. I guess I get to call myself a senior now."

"Me, too." Pamela noticed he had gorgeous eyes, but when she realized she had been staring into them, she dropped her gaze in confusion.

"I know." He glanced around, as if looking for a seat. Then, even though the bus was nearly empty, he dropped into the seat next to her.

Pamela felt little tingles along her thigh where their legs touched. After a silence that seemed to last forever, Ben cleared his throat and said, "Are you an artist? I noticed you were drawing before."

Pamela felt her cheeks color. Most people used the word *artist* to mean anyone who fooled around with paints and canvases, but not her. She had grown up thinking of the term as an honor that had to be earned. She didn't have the nerve to call herself an artist, not yet anyway, and she never knew what to say when people asked if she was one.

"I'm going to be the arts counselor," she answered, hedging his question. "I'm really looking forward to it. How about you?"

"Wilderness survival. Well, it's actually nature study. I'm so nervous I can't believe it. I've always been fascinated by science, but teaching it is something else. What if one of the kids brings me a bug and asks me what it is? What do I do then?"

"Take out your field guide and teach him how to look it up," Pamela said sensibly. "Then you'll both know what it is, and the next time he can find out for himself."

He was looking at her openmouthed. "Hey," he said. "What a great idea! Why didn't I think of it myself?"

"I'm sure you would have before long."

"You must have done this before, right? That's why you're so cool and confident."

She thought of all the anxieties about the job that had been plaguing her for days, and couldn't keep from smiling. "I don't feel so confident, if you want to know the truth, but I'm glad I look that way. I've never worked at a camp before, but this spring I gave an art workshop at Garfield House, in Geogretown."

"The halfway house? I was there last Christmas, working on Jonathan's homeless campaign."

"Really? Me, too! I knew I'd seen you somewhere besides school. Anyway, when I started giving the workshop, I was scared silly. But one of the other volunteers gave me some good advice. He said that it didn't matter if I wasn't the world's greatest expert on my subject, as long as I was willing to share what I know with people who know even less. I had to learn to feel okay about saying 'I don't know.' It wasn't easy, but once I did it I felt a lot more relaxed about facing my classes. I didn't have to keep up a front anymore."

"Hmm," Ben said thoughtfully. He looked doubtful.

His expression made her smile. "Well, there's another way to go," Pamela said. "You can always spend the next couple of days learning everything there is to know about nature."

"Now you're making fun of me," he said in a mock-plaintive voice. "And after I've been so open, confiding in you and all. Is that fair? Is that kind?"

Her smile widened into a grin. "I don't know," she replied. She turned away to glance out the window. "Hey, see that tree over there in the middle of the meadow? Is that some kind of oak?"

For a moment Ben looked startled and confused. Then he grinned back at her. "Gee, I don't know," he said. "Why don't we look it up?"

The other counselors turned to stare as they both cracked up.

Frank Tedesco, the camp director, taught English at Kennedy High during the year. Pamela had been in his class sophomore year, and as he walked to the front of the little circle of counselors, he gave her a nod. She had to fight not to yawn. Her dawn rising was starting to have an effect. What she really wanted was to curl up somewhere and take a nap, but this was definitely not the time or place. Camp counselors were supposed to be alert, eager, and full of energy. The very thought of being full of energy tired her out.

As Frank began his welcoming speech, she took out her pen and opened her notebook, intending to jot down all the important points. But then her thoughts drifted back to the bus ride and Ben. No boy had affected her in such a way since Matt. She tuned out Frank's speech and began sketching Ben's profile. He really was good-looking, with his strong jaw and well-defined cheekbones. His lips had a soft, gentle look about them and there were faint smile lines at the corners of his eyes. There was something incredibly cuddly about Ben, too, and Pamela couldn't help but wonder what it would feel like to be held in his arms.

She was so wrapped up in her thoughts of Ben that it was a moment before she realized Frank had stopped talking and was looking at her. She swallowed a couple of times and held back the impulse to pull the neck of her T-shirt up over her face. “Sorry,” she muttered. Everyone else had been paying rapt attention, and here she was, sketching away without the faintest idea of what Frank had been saying. She looked down at her lap and closed the sketchbook as unobtrusively as possible, but not before Ben got a look at it. Her cheeks turned bright pink, and she wanted to sink through the floor. She looked everywhere but at Ben, and when she could stand it no longer, she glanced at him out of the corner of her eye. He flashed her a huge smile that lighted up his face. She smiled back and again felt that familiar warmth shoot through her.

Chapter 2

Elise Hammond woke up just as the front door closed. Her father was on his way to work. As usual, he had tried to close the door quietly, but her bedroom was right over the front hall and the door always gave a curious squeak just before it latched itself.

She stretched her arms in the air and yawned. It felt very strange, almost sinful, to lie in bed on a weekday without worrying about being late for school. How long would it take her to get used to it? About two more days, she suspected, laughing to herself. Not that she really intended to stay in bed this morning — she had so many things she wanted to do — but it was nice to know that she could if she wanted to.

She tossed back the sheet and bounced out of bed. She glanced out the window just as a yellow school bus came down Everett Street from the direction of the park. As it began to slow down, the door of Ben's house flew open, and Ben came dashing down the steps, waving frantically. Elise smiled fondly as she watched him board the bus, but when it pulled out of sight, a wave of loneliness washed over her.

Ever since she was five or six years old, she and Ben and the other kids on the block had been meeting every morning for the walk to school. In past years, the only difference that summer had made was that they met a little later in the day and went to the park or over to somebody's house instead of to school. But they were older now, and their lives were changing. Steve Corbett was leaving in a couple of weeks to spend the summer with a cousin in Arizona. Sally Metcalfe had already left for Maine, where she was going to work as a waitress in a seaside resort hotel. And today marked the start of Ben's job as a counselor at Camp Woodlands.

He was the one she really cared about. She and Ben had always been best friends, ever since the days when they took turns giving each other pushes in his backyard swing. Over the winter, though, they had discovered that their feelings about each other had changed into something much deeper. It wasn't easy to be in love with someone you knew so well as a friend, but who said love was ever easy? It had taken time, a lot of serious discussions, and more than a few tears to work out the problems, but they had done it. By now they were as comfortable with each other as any couple she knew, even those who had been going together for a year or more.

She took her time getting dressed. There was no particular hurry — all she had on her schedule for the day was her volunteer work at Children's Hospital, and that didn't start until midafternoon.

Her mother was just finishing her cereal and coffee when Elise came into the kitchen. "Good morning," she said as she stood up to take her dishes to the sink. "How does it feel to be at liberty for a change?"

"Strange," Elise replied in a hollow voice. "Very strange." Her new diet called for nothing but fresh fruit until noon, so she found an apple in the fridge and started to slice it.

"Don't worry," her mother said with a laugh, "it's easy to get used to. Oops, I'd better dash. Fridays are always especially busy days for some reason. Will you be home for dinner?"

Elise shook her head. "I'll be at the hospital all afternoon. I'll get a bite at the cafeteria."

Her mother smiled. "All right, then, I'll see you tonight. Have a good day, sweetheart."

Elise sat at the kitchen table and poked at the apple slices with a fork. How much longer could she go on working as a volunteer? She had put off thinking about that question for as long as she could, but she needed to come to a decision in the next few days.

The program was really important, and the children really needed and appreciated it. It wasn't hard for her, either, and she enjoyed it. She loved telling them stories and jokes and playing games with them. Some of them were so brave that they almost made her ashamed.

So the work was definitely worthwhile, and she liked it. The problem was, did she have the *right* to do it? Was she carrying her share of the family load? Her older sister, Delayne, was in college now, and everybody knew how expensive *that* was. Delayne was working in an exclusive department store this summer selling cosmetics, trying to earn some of next year's tuition. No one had even hinted that Elise ought to get a real job, too, but she couldn't help thinking it. She had actually had an offer to work as a cashier in a Mexican restaurant, but when the job had fallen through, she hadn't even looked for another paid position.

She wouldn't have any trouble finding a job. Most of the stores at the mall and the fast-food places in town had help-wanted signs in their windows. The pay wasn't much, and the work was pretty dull, but at least she'd be bringing in something. She wouldn't be able to go on with her work with the kids if she had a job, though. She wouldn't have the time or the energy. Besides, it might be selfish of her, but she wanted to have *some* time for fun this summer. This was her first summer being in love, and she didn't want to waste it. She meant for it to be a summer she would remember the rest of her life.

The telephone was ringing as Elise was returning from the grocery store later that morning.

She walked a little faster, then set down her bag of groceries while she fumbled for her key. By the time she opened the door, the telephone had fallen silent. She looked at it for a moment, as if expecting it to start up again, then shrugged, and carried the groceries to the kitchen. If it was important, the caller would try again.

After putting the food in the refrigerator, she spent a couple of moments looking over the "Don't Forget" list. This was where her family kept reminders of tasks that needed to be done but not at any particular time. She didn't have enough self-confidence to reglue the leg on the broken dining room chair or enough time to straighten and dust the attic, but she could certainly manage to wash the living room windows before lunchtime.

She found the spray bottle of glass cleaner and a roll of paper towels and set to work. As she rubbed at the streaks left by the spray, her reflection stared back at her. Was there just a tiny hint of dissatisfaction in that face? What could she possibly be unhappy about? It was summer, school was out for two months, and she was going to have a wonderful time with the boy she had known and loved forever and ever. Or was that part of the problem? She knew Ben better than anyone in the world, maybe even better than she knew herself. When they talked, she had to stop herself from completing his sentences for him. But was it possible to know somebody *too* well, so well that the mystery, the romance, evaporated like the spray on the windowpane, leaving nothing but a gray film?

Elise was shocked by the direction of her thoughts. She and Ben were in love with each other. So what if she didn't feel herself tremble when he came near, the way she had a few months before when they were first discovering their love? So what if the idea of stealing one of his mittens and putting it under her pillow, as she had done back in February, made her want to laugh instead of sigh? She and Ben were a couple, and she was very happy.

She suddenly noticed that she had been polishing the same pane for two or three minutes. It was time to pay attention to what she was doing, instead of wallowing in all these depressing thoughts. Otherwise she would never get the windows done.

Washing the insides was a breeze, but the outsides were another matter. She was perched on the windowsill, hanging on with one hand and stretching up with the other to rub off a stubborn streak, when the telephone rang again. As she turned her head at the sound, her hand slipped off the windowframe. An awful instant later, she was hanging upside down in the shrubbery. She did a half-somersault and scrambled down to the ground, then stood there trying to catch her breath. She hadn't fallen far, and except for a few scratches on her arms she didn't think she was hurt. She was determined to go back inside and finish her task.

Throwing her shoulders back, she marched around to the front door and gave it a shove. Nothing happened. Of course not; it was locked. She pushed and pulled and rattled the knob, but she knew very well that it was useless. She always kept the doors locked when she was alone in the house. She wrinkled her nose in disgust and began to walk a circuit of the house, hoping for an inspiration. And there it was, only a few feet away, the open window she had taken her tumble from.

The only difficulty was that the sill was about six feet from the ground. She wriggled through the bushes and stood at full stretch. She could touch the top surface of the sill with her fingertips and even get a bit of a grip on it, but when she tried to pull herself up, her fingers slipped off. She set her jaw, took a deep breath, and tried to jump up. This time she got both hands onto the sill, but before they could find anything to grip, she had fallen back.

Her palms hurt. She stood rubbing them on her jeans and trying to think. Then she remembered the ladder in the shed behind the garage. She turned and strode purposefully around to the back of the house.

As she was passing the kitchen window, the telephone began to ring again. She scowled in its direction and muttered, "Oh, shut up!" To her surprise, it did.

Matt Jacobs was driving along Everett Street, going home for lunch, when he noticed someone creeping through the shrubbery in front of one of the houses. He slowed to a crawl and kept watching. A few moments later, the figure reappeared carrying a ladder and propped it against the side of the house near an open window. A burglar! He hit the brakes and tried to decide what to do. Shout? Chase the burglar himself? Go for the police?

While he was still debating and reaching for the door handle, the burglar looked in Matt's direction, saw him, and scurried through the window. A moment later, the window was slammed closed.

Matt laughed to himself and put the car in gear. The "burglar" was actually Elise Hammond, a fellow Kennedy student. Unless she had turned to a life of crime, she must have been climbing into her own house. He laughed again. What a sight! She had looked around so guiltily before scooting up that ladder. Matt drove on, his mind filled with images of Elise, the cutest burglar he had ever seen.

The lunch dishes were washed, dried, and returned to the cabinet. Elise strolled into the living room and admired the way the sunlight streamed in through the spotless windows. The day was almost as perfect as the windows: a cloudless, deep blue sky, bright with sunshine. If only the fine weather held through the weekend. She and Ben had talked about going for a bike ride on Saturday, and Sunday was Laurie Bennington's big jump-into-summer party at her father's house on the eastern shore. It promised to be one of the biggest events of the year.

The telephone rang. She walked quickly back to the kitchen and picked it up on the second ring.

"Hello?"

"Elise?" a familiar voice asked. "It's Virginia Coggins." Virginia ran the volunteer program at the hospital.

"Oh, hi," Elise said cheerfully.

"I'm glad I caught you. I have to be away from the hospital this afternoon, but I wanted to ask you something. Would you be able to put in a few more hours, maybe take on a little more responsibility during the summer?"

Elise's thoughts raced. How could she possibly take on more duties? Only that morning she had been thinking that she ought to leave the program altogether and get a paying job. "Um," she began, "I don't know — "

"You're one of our most experienced volunteers," Virginia continued, "and the children in the surgical ward can't wait for your next visit. What I would love to see you do, if you can manage it, is come in five afternoons and evenings a week. You could spend part of the time on the ward and part of it helping to train our newer volunteers. I can't offer you much over the minimum wage, so I'll understand if you say no, but you would be a big help to the program, Elise. And to the children, of course."

"Oh, Virginia," Elise began. "I wouldn't dream of saying no. I'd love to do it."

"Great! I'll leave you a memo with all the details, and we can talk it over when I see you tomorrow."

Elise hung up the phone and could barely keep from hopping up and down. She had been right. It was going to be an incredible summer.

Chapter 3

The automatic door opened with a faint sigh. The warm air was like a second wall just beyond the glass. Laurie Bennington paused to adjust the neckline of her swimsuit top, then stepped out into the sunlight and opened her arms wide in relief. The air-conditioning in the supermarket had been set high enough to give her goosebumps. Walking down the frozen food aisle had practically turned her lips blue.

"Which way?" a voice said.

She looked back. The delivery boy was waiting just behind her in the doorway with her two cartloads of groceries.

She pointed to the left. "The red convertible over there," she said. "Just put it all in the backseat, please."

As she followed him across the parking lot, she

wondered how she was going to unload all her purchases by herself. Where was Dick Westergard when she needed him? She couldn't believe that anyone would *want* to spend two weeks of summer vacation at a computer camp in Maine. At least she didn't have to worry about his being distracted up there, though. What computer nerd could compete with Laurie Bennington? She sensed that he was also eager to be someplace new, almost anyplace, as long as it wasn't Rose Hill. He hadn't even seemed that bothered by the fact that leaving Rose Hill meant leaving *her* as well.

"Nice car," the delivery boy said as he set one of the bags on the floor behind the driver's seat. Laurie tossed her head disdainfully. He didn't look a day over fourteen, though she had to admit he had nicely developed biceps. Probably the result of lifting groceries all day long.

"I bet you're throwing a party, right?"

"What gave you that brilliant idea?" she replied. She had meant to be sarcastic, but somehow it managed to come out sounding coy.

"Half a dozen giant bags of potato chips," he said cheerfully.

"I happen to like potato chips," Laurie said. "A lot."

His grin widened. "About a hundred paper plates. The expensive ones. Are you a nut for paper plates, too?"

"Okay," she conceded, "I am having a party. Not that it's any of your business."

"Well, excu-u-u-use me!" He lifted another bag out of the cart and glanced over his shoulder at Laurie. "Can I come? Pretty please?"

He looked at her with such pitiful eyes she had to smile. "Of course not. I'm only inviting my friends. You'd feel out of place."

"You mean your friends aren't as good-looking as I am?" he cracked.

"I mean they're too mature to stand around a parking lot making dumb remarks while forty pounds of ice melt! Now would you mind putting the rest of that stuff in my car?"

As he placed another bag of groceries into the backseat, he said, "Is it a beach party? I hope you bought insect repellent. The other day this skinny kid was attacked by horseflies. He hasn't been back to the beach since."

"I don't think we'll have that problem."

"You might," he replied, eyeing her low-cut swimsuit top. "What about suntan lotion? People who don't live around here don't realize how fast you can work up a really good burn. What you need is to invite someone local, sort of an expert adviser."

"Just finish up here and buzz off," Laurie said with exasperation. But she straightened her shoulders, took a deep breath, and tossed her head in a way she knew was alluring. The boy was so busy watching her he almost dropped one of the bags.

"Hey, something's dripping," he said suddenly.

"Oh, no," she moaned. "The ice cubes!"

"I'll put it on the floor, but you'd better be careful when you pick it up. You don't want the sack to break on you. Hey," he added, "maybe I can come home with you, to help you unload. It's nearly my lunch break. We could do a lot in an hour."

"Oh, please. Give me a break!" she exclaimed, slipping into the driver's seat.

"Here," she said, reaching into her pocket for a dollar bill. "Don't spend it all in one place," she added, backing out of her space.

As the camp van bumped along the swerving coast road, Dick Westergard leaned forward and stared out the open window. Maine certainly looks like Maine, he told himself.

The scene that rolled past could have been out of a travel movie. Tall pines lined the road, their cones still summer green. When the road curved by the shore, Dick could see dark, jutting rocks splashed by the white foam of rolling ocean waves.

"It's as beautiful up here as everyone says," he thought. If only Laurie could have been there with him to see it, too.

He had been thinking about Laurie a lot during the long van ride to the camp. He realized he missed her more than he thought he would. Sure, he had seen her the night before. But that was a lot of miles ago!

Dick smiled. The idea of Laurie Bennington coming along with him to a two-week computer camp was kind of funny. With her restless energy and short attention span, Laurie couldn't sit and stare at a computer monitor for two minutes, let alone two weeks!

His smile faded as he remembered how Laurie had turned her incredible energy against him. In the fall of their junior year, she had run against him for vice president of Kennedy High. And what a campaign she had waged. In the end, he won the election — and he won her, too. He realized he really cared about her. She realized she had found someone as confident and as independent as she was. They had been going together ever since.

The van hit a pothole, jarring Dick from his thoughts of Laurie. He looked around the van. Most of the other kids were ignoring the incredible scenery. They had their noses buried in computer manuals and programming guides.

They all think they're going to win the programming competition, Dick thought. *Too bad. They might as well close their books and enjoy the scenery. Because I'm going to win it with one hand tied behind my keyboard.*

Dick approached every project with the same confidence. He wasn't boastful. He never showed off. He was just the kind of person who could handle anything he set his mind to. Sure, part of his confidence came from his good looks, his winning smile, his dark, friendly eyes. But part of it came from knowing that good looks can only take you so far. The rest you have to do with brain power.

The van turned off the road onto a narrow gravel path. The path led up a sloping hill, lined with fragrant pine trees. The trees ended suddenly, and two rows of small wooden cabins came into view.

"Everybody out," the driver called, swinging open the door.

Dick climbed out of the van along with the others, and stretched his arms. It felt good to stand up. He took a deep breath of the cool, piny air, and looked around.

The hill continued to slope upward past the cluster of small cabins. At the top stood a three-storied Victorian mansion, painted bright yellow with white trim and shutters. The bright color made the stately old house look unreal, almost like something out of a cartoon. Dick thought it looked like an eighty-year-old woman wearing a prom dress designed for the junior prom!

"Welcome to Disney World," he said, but no one laughed. The other kids were all scrambling to retrieve their suitcases and backpacks from the baggage compartment in the back of the van.

Dick searched through the pile, thinking about how odd it was that the one-hundred-fifty-year-old house on the hill was filled with all of the latest computer equipment. He picked up the brown case (his mother had packed for him that morning) and began to walk toward the cabins.

"Hey — wait. I think that's my bag."

He turned quickly at the sound of the voice and found himself staring at one of the most beautiful girls he'd ever seen. Her shoulder-length auburn hair caught the soft rays of the late afternoon sun and seemed to sparkle and shimmer around her perfect face. Her eyes were dark green, flecked with gold, and they were staring into his.

"I — uh — sorry," was all he was able to say. He put the heavy bag down on the ground.

She continued to stare for a few seconds, as if studying him. Then she looked down at the bag. "Oh. Wow. I'm the one who's sorry. That's not my bag after all." She had a soft, breathy voice. It flashed in Dick's mind that maybe she had practiced making her voice so soft and breathy because it sounded sexy.

"Do you want it?" Dick joked. "Here. It's yours." He grinned at her.

She laughed, a breathy laugh. Her full lips formed a pout. "No. Thanks, anyway. I'd better find my own."

She tilted her head and looked at him again, slowly, calculatingly. "Hey, you know — you don't *look* like a computer nerd," she said, smiling warmly.

"Roxanne." Another girl, a thin, delicate-looking blonde, said disapprovingly, "You're not going to get very far here if you refer to everyone as computer nerds."

Roxanne shrugged, her eyes still on Dick.

"But I *am* a computer nerd," Dick told her. "These aren't my real looks. This is how I *really* look." He stuck his teeth out over his lower lip and crossed his eyes.

"Much better," Roxanne said, laughing that breathy laugh again, her beautiful green eyes seeming to laugh, too. "Now I believe you really belong in this camp."

"That's not very nice," the blonde girl said, shaking her head. She was very pretty, too, in a more subtle way. But she seemed so pale next to Roxanne. "Do you think I look like a computer nerd, too?"

"Of course not, Frankie," Roxanne said. "I don't hold it against you that you're into computers. You're normal in every other way."

"Gee, thanks for the great compliment," Frankie said sarcastically.

"What are best friends for?" Roxanne replied, staring at Dick.

"I'm Dick Westergard," he said, looking past her, watching a counselor, an older guy in jeans and a gray sweat shirt, coming down the hill, clipboard in hand.

"I thought so," Roxanne replied.

"What?" That reply got Dick's attention back. "You know me?"

"Oh . . . maybe I've heard some things about

you," Roxanne said coyly. "Frankie and I go to Stevenson. I'm Roxanne Easton. She's Frankie Baker."

"Oh," Dick frowned. "Two Stevenson girls, huh?" Stevenson was one of Kennedy High's biggest rivals. "We creamed you in the state playoffs last winter." He couldn't resist.

"Oh, really?" Roxanne said, shrugging. "I'm not into sports much."

"Roxanne is into a *different* kind of sports," Frankie said, and then looked embarrassed at her own joke.

"Don't pay any attention to her. She's a computer nerd," Roxanne said, giving her friend a playful shove.

"I guess you're not into sports or computers," Dick said. "Why did you come to this computer camp?"

"My mom was doing her spring housecleaning in the summer," Roxanne said. "And I was one of the things she cleaned out."

"It wasn't quite that bad, Rox," Frankie said.

"Let's put it this way," Roxanne continued, "She didn't want me hanging around."

"But why computer camp?" Dick insisted.

"Well, warmhearted Mom said that I had to spend at least part of the summer in some sort of school. You know, improving my mind."

"That means not thinking about boys for a few seconds," Frankie added.

Roxanne ignored her this time. "She said I had to take some sort of a course. Or else."

"Or else?"

"Or else I have to go to boarding school in the fall. So . . . when Frankie said she was coming up here for two weeks, I decided to tag along. I figured at least it would be almost bearable with my best friend along."

"Almost bearable?" Frankie cried. "Gee, thanks a *lot*, Rox!"

Roxanne started to say something, but the counselor with the clipboard interrupted their conversation. "Bunk assignments, bunk assignments," he called. "Everyone else but you is on their way to a cabin. You three going to sleep out here? I wouldn't advise it. It gets pretty cold up in these parts, even in the summer."

"I think we'd prefer indoor accommodations," Dick told him. Roxanne and Frankie laughed.

The counselor pointed them to their bunks. Dick gave the two girls a little wave and headed off to his cabin, lugging his suitcase in one hand and his duffel bag in the other.

After a few steps, he turned and watched Roxanne and Frankie walking to their cabin. "You know, Frankie," he heard Roxanne say in her breathy voice, "with *him* around, these two weeks might be even better than bearable. In fact, they could be really interesting."

Chapter 4

Elise took three quick steps to her left, pulled the racquet back ready to swing, and planted her feet. The bright yellow ball struck the court a half dozen feet in front of her and bounced just the way she had expected it to. She twisted at the waist and put everything into the stroke, not just power, but judgment and control. She knew even before the solid *thunk* that it had all gone exactly right. Elise moved toward the center of the court, poised in position to hit the return. She reveled in the feel of the already hot sun on her bare arms, the light breeze that ruffled her hair, and the exhilaration that came from really using her muscles.

The ball cleared the net by about an inch, zoomed crosscourt, and hit the green composition surface just inside the line. Ben, caught totally by surprise, straightened up and watched it go by with an expression of disgust on his face. Then he turned back and called, "Out. That's deuce."

"What!" Elise began indignantly. "That shot was in and you know it! If you think — " She finally noticed the grin on his face and broke off.

"Just trying to keep the game going," he explained as he walked toward the net. "That was set point, in case you hadn't noticed."

She gave him a mischievous smile. "Want a rematch, fella?"

"You've got to be kidding." He found his towel and began to wipe his face and neck. "After you took me six-one? Next time we play, you're going to have to wear ankle weights, handcuffs, and a blindfold. Maybe then I'll have a fair chance."

Her smile broadened. She and Ben had been playing tennis together for years, and he had always been the stronger player. He had never had Elise's accuracy or grace, but most of the time he beat her.

Over the past few months, however, things had changed radically. Thanks to a tennis class at school and some extra coaching from her dad, who had once played for his college team, she had sharpened her game a lot, adding power without losing accuracy. Gradually she had pulled even with Ben, and lately she had been winning consistently. He still had a more powerful stroke, but that didn't win him points as long as she kept putting the ball where he couldn't get to it.

She pulled off her headband and shook her

hair free. "Loser makes the lemonade, right?"

"I don't remember that rule. I thought you always made the lemonade."

"That was because I always lost." She zipped the cover of her racquet closed and picked up her shoulder bag. "I'll show you how, if you've forgotten," she added, then tried to dodge as he grabbed for her.

Suddenly his arms were around her waist and his lips were brushing her neck just below her left ear. A shiver ran down her spine. With a sigh, she closed her eyes and leaned back against him, wishing that this moment would go on and on. But almost at once, he released her and straightened up. "We'd better go," he said. "Someone else'll want the court."

Wordlessly she looked around the deserted park. Who could possibly want the court? He was acting shy again, that was all. Why did he always find it so hard to show his emotions?

Ben turned pink, but the determined look stayed on his face. He slung his tennis bag over his shoulder, then held out his hand, palm up. "Friends?"

Elise hesitated for a split second, but her irritation with him seemed so childish and pointless that she couldn't hang on to it. "Friends," she said, and took his hand.

A few minutes later they were sitting on the grass in his backyard, sipping their iced lemonades. Elise was just finishing the tale of her misadventures cleaning the living room windows.

When she described her fall into the bushes, followed by the discovery that she had locked herself out of the house, he laughed uproariously.

"But it all turned out okay," she concluded. "Isn't that great about getting paid for the hospital job? It's almost too good to be true."

"Yeah, it does sound like a good deal," Ben said, leaning back on his elbows and looking toward the garage. "But it's too bad you couldn't have worked it out to have your evenings free. I can't believe you really have to work five afternoons *and* evenings.

Elise toyed with her shoelaces. "Well, I couldn't have turned her down, Ben. The offer was just too good. I love the work, and getting paid for it, well. . . ."

"I know you couldn't have said no, but I can't help thinking about how it blows our evenings, that's all. You won't be getting home until eight or nine, and if I have to be up before seven the next morning, we're not going to have very much time together."

"I know," she said softly, touched by his concern. "But we'll really enjoy the time we do have, won't we? And we'll still have some weekends to be together."

"Sure," he repeated, but something in his tone made her study his face. Why was he avoiding her eyes?

"We will, won't we?" she demanded.

"Well. . . ." He plucked a blade of grass and stared down at it as if it fascinated him.

"Well what?"

"The thing is, I'm going to have to do a lot of preparation for my work at camp, putting in time at the library and the zoo and the natural history museum. I'll be working all week long, right? So that just leaves Saturday and Sunday for the other stuff."

"I wouldn't mind spending the day at the zoo with you," Elise said. "I bet we'd have fun."

Ben refused to look up from his blade of grass. "Oh, sure," he replied. "We ought to do that someday. But right now I'm talking about work. I'd have to take notes, talk to some of the staff, and stuff like that. It might get boring for you." Just as she was about to accuse him of not wanting her around, he added, "Besides, you know I can't concentrate on anything else when you're around. I love you too much."

For a moment she felt herself begin to melt. "I love you, too," she said. "But that's not the point. Are you trying to tell me that you're going to be busy with your nature study work every Saturday and Sunday this summer?"

"No, not *every* Saturday and Sunday. Just a lot of them."

"But, Ben," she demanded, "when are we going to have any time to be together?"

"We'd have our evenings if you weren't doing so much volunteer work."

"Ben!" She didn't know whether she felt more hurt or indignant. Didn't he realize the importance of what she was doing, not only for the children in the hospital, but for *herself*? She looked at him for a long time before saying, "I can't believe you meant that the way it sounded. I know how upset you are that we can't have more time together. I'm upset, too. I was really looking forward to being with you a lot." Her eyes began to sting, but she forced back her tears. She didn't want to start crying in front of him, not now. "I'd better go home," she said quickly. "I want to take a shower. Come over later if you're not too busy." She couldn't keep the touch of sarcasm out of her voice.

"I will," Ben replied. But still he refused to look at her. Elise walked away with the feeling that the summer wasn't quite going to live up to her expectations. Not after such a bad start.

Laurie opened the sliding glass door and stepped out onto the deck. The sun was blazing, but a breeze off the water kept the air cool and pleasant. She pulled the loose robe up over her head and tossed it onto a chair. Under it she was wearing a brand-new bathing suit. It rode high at her hips and low at the bust, and the skin-tight Lurex in between made an intricate pattern of panels and cutouts. In the store mirror it had looked really hot, but now she realized how impractical it was. If she wore it more than once a week, she was going to finish the summer with a tan that made her look like a piece of modern art, all stripes and whorls and odd little blobby shapes. Yuck.

A flight of wooden stairs led down to the beach. She paused at the top to look over the scene. The water was an intense blue, made darker by contrast with the white foam of the breakers and the white sails of offshore boats. Only a handful of swimmers were out, although off to the right in the direction of town, the sand was beginning to disappear beneath towels and umbrellas. It was still the very start of the season, too. By the middle of July, every weekend would be like that. Laurie didn't really mind. On weekdays she and her neighbors still had the beach pretty much to themselves.

She was studying the hollow just to the left of the stairs, wondering if it would be a good spot for a bonfire, when a movement caught her eye. She glanced up. A boy was running along the beach parallel to the water. His tanned chest and broad shoulders gleamed in the sunlight and his stomach muscles rippled with each easy breath. He looked as if he could keep up that long, loping stride forever. As he drew even with the stairs, he looked over and noticed her. Their eyes met, and she felt her breath catch. He gave her a grin and a casual wave, then disappeared up the beach at the same steady pace.

Laurie kept watching even after he was out of sight. "*Quel* hunk," she murmured in her best Miss Piggy voice. It was purely an aesthetic judgment. She was in love with Dick Westergard, and he was in love with her. What did it matter that Dick had gone off so blithely for the summer, with so little thought of her? She had absolutely no interest in any other boy, even if he did look like a Greek statue. She turned away with a tiny hint of regret that she might never see him again.

As she walked back to the house, she found herself humming the theme from *Chariots of Fire*.

Chapter 5

Pamela stepped back from the easel and stared critically at the canvas. The dark red vase filled with yellow sunflowers was coming along, and she was doing well at catching the shadows in the folds of the tablecloth, but something was wrong in the lower left corner.

Green, that was it. She had somehow overlooked the faintly greenish tinge in the glass of the wine bottle. There were missing highlights, too. The vase had a terrific three-dimensional feel to it, but the bottle looked as if it had been snipped out of construction paper. She reached for the big tube of titanium white and squeezed a line of it onto her palette.

The whine of a passing motorcycle broke her concentration. She blinked, lowered her brush, and glanced around the room. Suddenly she noticed her clock radio and frowned. Ten-thirty? It couldn't be. But her watch, once she found it under a couple of painting rags, said the same. Where had the time gone? She had come upstairs after breakfast to do a little painting, but she had known that she wouldn't be able to work for long. She and Matt were going on a picnic today. He was supposed to come by for her at eleven, and she still hadn't put together their lunch.

She quickly cleaned the palette and washed her brushes, then hurried down to the kitchen. Fortunately she had boiled the potatoes the night before and left them in the fridge. It didn't take long to cut them up and stir in mayonnaise, sour cream, a little mustard, a dash of cayenne pepper, and a few capers. After tasting the mixture, she added some fresh dill from the window box, then transferred the potato salad to a plastic container.

How strange that she had gotten so totally involved in her work that she'd managed to forget their date completely. It was probably a good sign. For a while, when she and Matt first started going out together, she hadn't been able to paint at all. Whenever she stood at her easel, all she could think of was his face, the feel of his hands, and the lonely hours she had to endure before she saw him again.

She put together a baked ham and cheddar cheese sandwich, then reliable peanut butter and jelly for herself. For Matt she repressed a faint shudder and made his favorite concoction, peanut butter and sliced banana with mayo. Making it was bad enough, but sitting by while he ate it. . . !

She had packed the food and sodas in the cooler and was hunting for napkins and plastic forks when Matt tapped on the kitchen door. The sight of his face through the glass brought a smile to her lips. How had she managed to live so much of her life without being in love? It seemed impossible to imagine. She pulled the door open, and he caught her in a bear hug that lifted her off the floor.

She wrapped her arms around his neck and gave him a warm kiss. Then she drew her head back and said with a smile, "Let me down while I still have a few ribs left."

He let go so quickly she almost fell. "Sorry," he said in his gruff voice. "I've missed you."

"Me, too." She rested her cheek against his shoulder for a moment, then gave him a teasing glance. "It's been a whole day since we saw each other, hasn't it?" she said. "I'm lucky it wasn't a week or two. You might have squeezed me into jelly."

"Grrr — good idea." He started to tighten his arms again, but she laughed and wriggled free.

"It looks like a perfect day for a picnic." She checked the contents of the cooler one more time, then added some apples, oranges, and raisins before closing it. "Ready?"

"Uh-huh." As he picked up the cooler, he added, "By the way, I've got a big surprise for you."

"You do?"

"Yep, it's outside. Come on."

She followed him out the door, around the corner of the house, and down the driveway. At the edge of the front yard he stopped. "So what do you think?" he demanded.

At first she didn't know what he meant. Then she realized that he had to be talking about the car. Matt always drove an old yellow and red Camaro that he had restored beautifully, but it was not in its usual spot at the curb. In its place sat a battered convertible that looked as if it had narrowly escaped the wrecking ball. She could see that it had once been metallic bronze with white racing stripes, but now the predominant color was rust. Anyone trying to sell it would probably call it an antique, but a more honest name would be junk.

"Isn't it awesome?" Matt asked.

One side of the front bumper was held on with wire, and a long rip in the canvas top had been patched with cloth tape. "It certainly is," she replied, though she doubted if he meant the same thing by awesome as she did. "Uh, what exactly is it?"

He led her down the front walk to the car. "It's a 1965 Mustang," he said proudly. He reached over to pat the air scoop that jutted up from the hood. "It's just about the hottest one I've ever seen, too. Somebody jerked the stock engine and put in a Cobra 289 with three carbs and a wicked cam. I bet it used to eat Olds 442's for breakfast!"

Going with Matt Jacobs and listening to his

Popular Mechanics conversations with Jonathan had taught Pamela a lot. She had a fairly clear idea of what he was talking about. Apparently this tired old heap had an unusually powerful engine under that jutting air scoop. Somehow she couldn't get excited about that. The yellow and red Camaro had been more than powerful enough for her, and it had been in a lot better shape, too. This car might still be able to go very fast, but it looked as if it might lose a wheel or some other vital part in the process.

"Well, what do you think?"

She hesitated. "Whose is it? Did you borrow it from someone?" She was afraid she knew the answer.

"No way!" Matt said indignantly. "It's mine! You know that guy I told you about, who's been after me for months to buy the Camaro? Well, I sold it to him and got the rest of the money from my uncle. I wasn't going to let a chance like this slip out of my hands."

"You mean this cost you more than the Camaro was worth? That doesn't sound fair. After all the work you'd done on it? You've had that car since you were fourteen."

He shrugged. "I know . . . and it *was* in good shape, but that's not what really counts. There wasn't anything special about it. It was the most popular model from a very popular year. There are still lots of them around. But an early Mustang ragtop is another story. It's a collector's item, practically a museum piece. And I bet there isn't another one anywhere with a 289 Cobra mill in it."

Pamela gave up. Matt was an intelligent guy. He certainly must have thought it over carefully before deciding to buy the Mustang. Maybe she would have made a different decision if it had been up to her, but so what? No matter how much she loved Matt, she couldn't really see things exactly the way he did. He was as pleased with the car as a little kid with a new bicycle, and she had no right to spoil it for him. Already her lack of enthusiasm was starting to make him feel unsure of himself. She could see it on his face.

"It's really something," she said finally. There wasn't anything dishonest about that, was there? "Are we going to take it on our picnic?"

"We'd better," he said with grim humor. "It's that or walk."

"Then I vote for the Mustang. We won't get far walking, not with the amount of stuff I packed in that cooler."

Pamela walked over to the car and reached for the door handle, but he grabbed her wrist. "Uh-uh," he said apologetically. "That's one of the first things I'm going to work on."

"What would have happened?" she asked curiously. "Would the handle have come off in my hand?"

"Probably not. But the door might have fallen on your foot." He laughed at her expression, then added, "Not really. I've got it wired shut. But why take chances? You'll have to come in on my side and scoot over."

Their destination, a tract of undeveloped parkland bordering the Potomac River, was a half-hour drive away. By the time they arrived, Pamela was sure she had never spent a more uncomfortable half-hour in her life. The car rocked and swayed and darted from one side to the other, and with every motion the sharp seat springs jabbed her through her clothes. Whenever they were moving, the engine roared deafeningly, and whenever they slowed to a stop, the brakes gave a piercing screech.

Terrible as the noises were, though, they weren't nearly as bad as the gasoline and exhaust fumes that filled the car. They couldn't even lower the top because it was broken. Pamela began developing an incredible headache even before they were out of Rose Hill. By the time Matt pulled off the road near the path to their private spot, the headache was no longer confined to the territory just behind her eyes. It had become a ribbon of pain that completely encircled her skull just above ear level and extended down either side of her neck into her shoulders.

The constant din had kept them from exchanging more than a few words during the drive, but Matt must have sensed her discomfort. As soon as they stopped, he gave her an apologetic look. "I did say it needed a lot of work," he said. "But you can see what a fantastic deal it was, can't you?"

Instead of answering, she looked away. She was feeling too out of sorts to work at being polite, but she didn't want to fight with him. What was the point?

She was hunting for the door handle when he said, "You have to come out this way. Remember? I'll get the cooler."

She wriggled into a half crouch and began to climb over the gear shift and the gap between the two bucket seats, when suddenly the floor seemed to give way under her foot. She let out a startled cry and fell back into her seat.

"What happened?" Matt asked, thrusting his head through her window. When he saw he said, "Oh, I forgot to tell you. The floorpan's rusted through in a few places. A lot of old Mustangs have that problem."

"I don't understand. You mean the car has holes in the floor?"

"Well . . . sort of."

"I could have poked my foot through the floor while we were going fifty miles an hour?"

He shook his head. "No. The holes aren't that big yet, and besides, the floor mat would have kept you from going through."

She was appalled. "Can't you fix it?" she asked helplessly.

"Oh, sure. A guy told me about a place in Delaware that makes replacements out of fiberglass, but they don't come cheap. I guess I'd better do a temporary fix on Monday with some Masonite, then order a new floorpan when I have the money. That might be a while, though. There's the car itself to pay for, too."

The path led through the woods a hundred yards or so to a clearing that overlooked the river. Years before, someone had put a wooden picnic table there. Though falling apart, it was still more or less usable. A little like the Mustang, Pamela thought as she laid out the plates and sandwiches, but not nearly as dangerous. Still, she wasn't going to dwell on that. It was time to talk about something else.

Matt must have felt the same way. "It's nice up here," he said. He walked over to the edge of the bluff and looked down at the water. "It's so quiet, and the air smells so clean."

She joined him and put her hand on his shoulder. He slipped an arm around her waist.

"Look at that bird," he continued. "I think it's some kind of hawk. Look how it stays up there, circling around and around without moving a feather. One of these days maybe I'll learn as much about birds and animals as I have about cars."

Just then, a chipmunk peeped out from the underbrush, studied them with bright eyes, and scampered across the clearing to the picnic table.

"Oh, no! The sandwiches!" Pamela exclaimed.

Too late. Half a sandwich was already disappearing into the bushes.

"What do chipmunks eat?" Matt asked as they hurried over.

"I don't know," she replied grimly. "They seem to like peanut butter." She checked the remaining half sandwich and added, "Especially with jelly."

"Don't worry," Matt said cheerfully, "you can share my peanut butter and banana if you like."

"That's what I was afraid of." She looked down at the rip in the plastic sandwich bag and started to laugh. "Did you see that little guy?" she demanded. "The bread was bigger than he was! How did he manage to carry it like that?"

Matt grinned. "If you saw a chance to grab enough meals for the next month, you'd manage, too. We'd better eat right away, before he spreads the news. Otherwise we might find ourselves feeding every chipmunk in the county!"

After lunch they sat down on a grassy spot on the hillside with a view of the wooded valley below. Pamela leaned back against Matt and felt his arm encircle her shoulders. She took his left hand in both of hers and stroked the fingers one by one, then kissed his fingertips. His arm tightened around her as he gently pulled her down next to him in the tall, fragrant grass. As his soft lips met hers, she looked up at the flawless sky and wondered if anyone had a right to be so happy. Then she closed her eyes and gave herself up completely to their embrace.

"I haven't told you anything about camp," Pamela said later, sitting up and brushing the hair out of her eyes. "I haven't met any of the kids yet, but I think it's going to be a lot of fun."

"How does it work?" Matt asked. "Will you be doing art full-time, or what?"

"Afternoons. Mornings, I'm a counselor like everybody else. I got to know some of the others yesterday, and they seemed like a nice bunch. You know Ben Forrest, don't you? He knows Jonathan."

"Sure, he's a science nut. He's always designing helicopters and stuff. Is he working there, too?"

"Uh-huh. He's the nature study counselor." She broke off at the *rat-tat-tat* of a woodpecker. It was somewhere nearby. She looked around but couldn't pinpoint the source of the sound. With a shrug she leaned back and said, "He's nervous about it, too. He thinks he has to know everything about his subject. I felt the same way when I started leading that class at Garfield House. Remember?"

Matt picked up a twig and bent it until it broke, then bent the two pieces again. He seemed more interested in the twig than in what she was saying.

She frowned and studied his face. Why wasn't he talking to her? Was she *that* boring?

She tried again. "I feel okay about the art classes, but I don't know how I'll handle the mornings. I don't even know any kids that age. Ben's lucky. He's got a couple of kid brothers, so he's really experienced with keeping them in line and involved. Isn't it great that I've got someone like him to go to for advice and encouragement?"

Matt nodded, then glanced at his watch. "Hey, it's later than I thought. We'd better go."

She looked at him in surprise. "Why? Don't we have all day?"

"Unh-uh. I said I'd cover for Phil at the station this afternoon. Didn't I tell you?"

She got to her feet. "No," she replied quietly, "you didn't."

"Oh. I thought I had." He was avoiding her eyes again. "Yeah, well, see, that's part of my deal with my uncle: he's going to pay me time-and-a half for filling in on weekends. The other guys, they're married — have families; they like to get away on summer weekends, so it works out fine all around."

"You mean you're going to be working at the gas station every weekend?"

He shifted from foot to foot. "Well, it's hard to say. It'll be a week-to-week kind of thing. But most weekends, I guess. It's a lucky break. I need the extra money to help pay for the Mustang."

She took his arm and turned him to face her. "What about tomorrow? It's Laurie's beach party, remember?"

"Of course I remember," he said indignantly. "Listen, don't worry, I worked it all out. Jonathan and Fiona will give you a ride. You can still have a fun time at the beach, even if I have to be back in Rose Hill pumping gas."

She shook her head. "Matt," she said, "I don't care that much about the beach, or Laurie's party, or any of that. I care about *you.* I was looking forward to our afternoon together and to going to the party with you and to being with you on weekends this summer. I'm disappointed, that's all. And I wish you hadn't waited so long to tell me about it."

"I didn't want to spoil our picnic."

She let out a sarcastic laugh. As far as she was concerned, the picnic was already spoiled. Still, why make things worse than they already were? "Come on," she said, holding out her hand, "let's pack up the things and start back. It's too bad you have to work weekends, but I guess it isn't the end of the world. We'll still have some evenings together, after I get back from day camp."

He suddenly looked very uncomfortable again.

"We *will,* won't we, Matt?"

"Um, the thing is, my uncle asked me to move over to the four-to-twelve shift starting next week. I would have said no, but it comes to more an hour, and with all the parts I need to buy for the car, not to mention paying him back for the loan. . . ." His voice trailed off.

"Matt," she said, her voice rising, "I do not believe what I'm hearing. You're going to be working every evening Monday through Friday, and weekends, too? *When am I going to see you?*"

His face reddened. "Look, Pamela, I don't like this any more than you do, but I've got to do it. It's my summer job."

She shook her head. "Yeah. You're working longer and worse hours because you want extra money for the Mustang. That's what it comes down to. You care more about that car than you do about me."

She turned away and started across the clearing, head high. Why were things with Matt starting to feel all wrong? Maybe she should never have started going out with him in the first place. But oddly enough, she knew she was arguing with him as a matter of principle. She didn't like playing second fiddle to his car. Truthfully, though, Matt's extra hours at the station would give her more time to paint and do things she really did want to do this summer. It didn't seem like that big a deal.

At the entrance to the path, Pamela turned back to look at Matt. He was still standing in the same place, looking upset and confused. Some demon made her say, "Come on. You don't want to be late for work, do you?"

Chapter 6

"Frankie?"

"Yes?"

"Can I ask you a technical question about computers?"

"Sure, Rox. What is it?"

"Well, how do you do all that typing on the keyboard without breaking your nails?"

Frankie slammed her notebook shut and tossed it at Roxanne. Both girls started to laugh.

"Hey, it's supposed to be Lights Out," a girl's voice called sleepily from the other side of the cabin.

"Put a sock in it," Roxanne said.

"What?!"

"She said, we'll be more quiet," Frankie offered, clicking off the little pocket light she was using to read the programming notes in her notebook. "We'll have to whisper," she whispered to her friend.

"No. I've got a better idea," Roxanne whispered back. "Put something on over your pajamas. Quick."

"Oh, no. I don't believe this," Frankie exclaimed. "You want to sneak out of the bunk on the *first* night?! No. N-O. Forget it, Rox. No way."

A few seconds later, the girls were creeping along the back wall of the cabin, shivering in the cold night air, walking across the pebbled path toward the trees under the pale, white summer moon.

"Everything smells so fresh and clean up here," Frankie said, still whispering even though there was no one around.

"Enough sensitive nature talk," Roxanne said. "What do you think?"

"Think? About what?" Frankie tripped over a twig, caught her balance, and kept walking, her sneakers crunching on the hard ground.

"You know. About him."

Frankie stopped and turned around. "I'm going back," she said. "I can't believe we're all this way from home, and you still only want to talk about boys."

"Not *boys*," Roxanne corrected her. "*Boy.* Dick Westergard. Mr. Soft Curly Hair and Brown Puppy Eyes."

"I'm going to throw up," Frankie said.

"Come off it, Frankie," Roxanne said impatiently. "You liked him, too. He's a fox, right?"

"Right," Frankie said quietly. "He seems like a really nice guy."

"What has *nice* got to do with it?" Roxanne joked. They both laughed.

They found two large tree stumps near the edge of the trees and sat down. The wind rustled the branches. Some kind of creature made crackling sounds as it scampered over the carpet of pine needles in the woods behind them.

"It's nice that you have a hobby," Frankie said, shivering. "Some people collect dolls or seashells. You collect boys."

Roxanne laughed. "It's a good thing we're such close friends," she said softly. "Otherwise, I might think you were putting me down."

"Oh, no. I wouldn't do that. You've been the same since fifth grade. You were boy-crazy then, and you're — "

"Now, wait a minute, Frankie. I'm not boy-crazy. Don't make me sound like a character in one of those silly romance books."

"*You're* the one who's always reading those, Rox. I certainly don't."

"Oh, no. Of course not. You're Miss Intellectual. Miss Computer Whiz. Well, did it ever occur to you that maybe I'm sincere? Maybe I'm really attracted to him. And I think he was really attracted to me. And maybe it could be the real thing this time?"

"But, come on, Rox," Frankie said, trying to remember how many times she'd heard her friend say the exact same words about other boys. "You know as well as I do that Dick already has a girl friend. Everyone knows he's going with that girl who ran against him in the student election at Kennedy — you know, that rich girl who lives in the enormous house that looks like something from *Gone With The Wind*?"

Roxanne turned and stared at the trees, all shades of gray under the pale moonlight. "Money isn't everything," she said quietly.

"But this girl is supposed to be really a knockout too," Frankie persisted.

"Well . . . money and looks aren't everything," Roxanne said. "Geography has to count for something."

"What do you mean?" Frankie asked suspiciously.

"I mean, I'm here — and she's *there*."

"I get it," Frankie said, shaking her head.

"You're a very smart girl," Roxanne told her.

"Yeah. That's me. Smart," Frankie said with unusual bitterness. "Smart doesn't seem to count as much as other things when it comes to getting guys."

Roxanne chuckled. "Well . . . having a fabulous body helps." She put a hand on her friend's shoulder. "Listen. Don't start feeling sorry for yourself, Frankie. You're very smart and you're very pretty, and guys would like you a lot if you ever showed any interest. But you keep your delicate little nose in books and in front of your computer monitor — so what do you expect?"

"I don't know. I don't want to talk about it," Frankie said. "I just don't want to be known my whole life only as Roxanne Easton's friend."

The two girls were silent for a while. The steady, insistent chirping of three frogs and crickets was the only sound. Frankie was regretting what she had just said. Roxanne was thinking of something else entirely.

"Uh . . . Frankie . . . speaking of being friends. . . ."

"Yeah?" Frankie was used to Roxanne thinking only of herself.

"Well . . . you know I just came up here to spend time with you. I'm really not into computers at all."

"I know, Rox. And I know what you're going to ask me, too."

"You do? What?"

"You're going to ask me if I'll do your computer project for you and get you through the course."

"You're smart. And you're a mind reader," Roxanne said. "Will you do it for me? Please?" She had a way of sounding like a lost little girl whenever she pleaded like that.

"Sure. No problem," Frankie said, wondering to herself why she put up with Roxanne. Immediately, she answered her own question. She put up with her in order to be known to everyone as Roxanne Easton's friend. "Let's go in. It's freezing out here," she said, standing up and wrapping her arms around herself, trying to shake out the cold.

"No, wait." Roxanne jumped up from the tree stump. "I just got an idea. Maybe after the computer session tomorrow afternoon Dick and I can go out for a little beach party."

"Wonderful idea," Frankie said, shivering. "Have a great time. Can we go in now?"

"No. Not yet." Roxanne had a devilish look on her face. "I have to go invite him. Come on." She started walking quickly along the path to the boys' cabins.

"Oh, no!" Frankie called after her. "No way. Sneaking out of the bunk on the first night of camp to have a chat is one thing. But sneaking over to the boys' cabins is — is — "

Roxanne was walking so quickly, Frankie lost sight of her in the darkness. She could hear her sneakers crunching over the pebbles, but she couldn't see her. "Hey, Rox — wait up!" Frankie ran to catch up with her friend.

A few moments later they were peeking into the window of Cabin B-3. "It's pitch-black in there," Roxanne said, sounding surprised.

"Big surprise," Frankie whispered. "Everyone is asleep in this camp but us."

"Well, then we'll just have to wake him up," Roxanne said. Before Frankie could stop her, she bent down, picked up a small stone, and heaved it at the closed cabin window.

Unfortunately, she threw it a little harder than

she had intended. The window shattered with a deafening crash.

A few seconds later, a boy with short blond hair and a very confused expression poked his head out of the now glassless window frame. "Hey! Visitors!" he yelled loudly. They could hear guys waking up, moving around inside the dark cabin. "Come on in, girls!" He stuck out a hand to help them through the window.

"You wish!" Roxanne sneered.

Frankie was too embarrassed to do or say anything. She hid in the shadows, hoping the boys couldn't see her.

"Party time!" the blond guy insisted.

"Get real," Roxanne said. "I didn't mean to wake you from your beauty rest. I'm looking for Dick Westergard."

"Who?"

"Dick Westergard. He's tall. Curly brown hair."

The blond guy disappeared, and a few seconds later, Dick poked his head through the window. He was still half asleep, and he looked just as confused as the first guy. "Hi, hi. What a nice surprise."

There were loud voices inside the cabin and a lot of raucous laughter. Frankie was mortified. She was furious at herself for following Roxanne. She knew that neither of them would live this down. But, of course, only she would care about that. Roxanne never worried about small things — like her reputation.

"I came to invite you to a beach party tomorrow afternoon after the computer session," Roxanne said, oblivious to all the loud remarks and jokes being made inside the cabin.

"Uh . . . great. Sounds great," Dick told her. "Thanks. Uh . . . who is giving this party?"

"I am," Roxanne said kittenishly.

"Oh. And who-all is invited?" Dick asked, waking up a little.

"You and me," she replied suggestively.

Even though he was barely awake, Dick did some quick thinking. Mainly he thought about Laurie. Here he was, away from her for only one day, and he was about to go off on a private — very private — beach party with this absolute fox who was obviously very interested in him.

No. It wasn't smart. And it wasn't right.

But still . . . he was going to be here in this camp in Maine for two weeks. It wouldn't hurt to be friendly and meet new people and. . . .

Suddenly, he realized that Roxanne wasn't alone. Peering into the shadows, he saw Frankie trying to make herself invisible behind her.

"Well? Will you come?" Roxanne asked breathily.

"Yeah. Sure," Dick said. He turned to Frankie. "You come, too. Okay?"

"What?" Frankie asked, startled.

"You come, too," Dick repeated. "I want you to. Really." She can be our chaperon and keep me out of any trouble, he told himself. Besides, she seems really nice.

Frankie looked at Roxanne. It was hard to see her expression in the darkness, but she knew Roxanne was probably not too pleased about Dick's invitation. "Yes. Okay. I'll come, I guess." What else could she say?

A few seconds later, the two girls were sneaking back along the path to their cabin. "Don't feel bad, Frankie," Roxanne was saying. "Dick and I will have a good time tomorrow even if you do tag along."

Chapter 7

On Sunday morning, Laurie took her list of things to do down to the beach and looked it over. There were a few last-minute chores to take care of, such as moving the cans of soda from the refrigerator to the tub and icing them down, but practically everything else was checked off. No wonder — she had been up working since seven. She wasn't in the habit of getting up so early, but she had been too excited to sleep. Not just excited, but anxious as well. This was the first time she had ever given a big party entirely on her own, without the help of her father's housekeeper. She couldn't believe how many details she had to take care of, and she couldn't avoid the suspicion that she had overlooked something terribly important.

If so, it was too late to fix now. Reassured by this fatalistic thought, she leaned back, closed her eyes, and let herself be lulled by the warmth of the sun and the sound of the waves. The checklist slipped from her fingers and fell to the sand. It was strange to think that her last real contact with Kennedy High, like her first, was going to be a big party. A lot had changed in two years, but she had remained famous for her great parties.

When she had moved to Rose Hill and enrolled at Kennedy at the start of her junior year, she had wanted only one thing: to be accepted as a leading member of the in-crowd at her new school. For that first big party, she had deliberately invited everyone who might help her toward that goal and had left out anyone who couldn't. She had had the latest music videos on the big projection TV, an extravagant spread of food, candle lanterns strung across the back garden and around the pool — all to make sure that on Monday morning the whole school would be talking about her.

It had worked, too. Before long she had gained an important position in student government, and she had had her own shows on WKND, the school radio station. Gradually, however, she began to see that she had been too busy trying to impress people to make any real friends.

This party was going to be different, because she had changed. She no longer felt the need to impress people, and she wasn't trying to get something from everyone the way she used to. All she wanted now was for her friends to have a lot of fun. Of course, she wanted to have a good time herself, too, and she still wanted her classmates to like her. But she knew now that she couldn't buy their friendship. It had to be earned.

Her thoughts drifted back to Dick and what a lonely summer was in store for her. What a drag it was that he had gotten that summer job in Maine. It certainly wasn't very flattering to think that he preferred the company of a lot of nerdy little computer whizzes to her.

Over the hiss of the waves she began to hear the slap-slap of feet on wet sand. The sound was drawing closer. She propped her Vuarnet sunglasses up on the top of her head and looked around. The boy she had privately nicknamed Apollo was running along the beach straight toward her. His thick hair gleamed golden in the sun, and the stark white of his nylon running shorts made his skin look golden, too. As he approached, he looked in her direction. His eyes were startlingly blue and his teeth were white and even.

"Nice day," she called out as he came even with her. She thought he might pause long enough for her to introduce herself and casually ask him to drop by her party later, but he merely smiled once more, waved, and ran on down the beach.

"Rats!" Laurie muttered. Surely she could find some way to get him to stop. Not that she really cared about someone she didn't know. He might even turn out to be a total creep. It was merely the challenge that mattered to her. She wasn't used to having handsome guys run past her with no more acknowledgment than a smile and a wave. Certainly not when she was lying on the beach in a skimpy Brazilian bikini.

She sat up, shaded her eyes, and stared in the direction of town. Was he likely to come by again, or had he been on the return leg of his run? What difference did it make anyway? She wasn't going to sit out in the sun waiting for him. That was a half-baked idea, and if she stayed out much longer, she was going to be a good deal more than half-baked.

A horn honked from the direction of the house. Startled, she glanced at her watch. She had totally forgotten that she was expecting a delivery of tables and chairs from the rental company. Oh, no! She hoped they weren't driving off by now because no one came to the door. She grabbed her towel, robe, and list, and ran quickly across the beach as if her feet were burning.

A horn honked from out front. Pamela walked over to her bedroom window, imagining for one moment that she would see Matt in his Camaro, there to take her to Laurie's beach party. But the street was empty. Of course it was. The Camaro now belonged to someone else, Matt was working at his uncle's gas station, and Jonathan and Fiona were taking her to the party.

She pressed her forehead against the window, welcoming the smooth coolness of the glass against her skin. She wanted to go away, to be by herself in some beautiful, lonely spot where she could paint and sketch and think seriously about what was going on between her and Matt. It might be boring at times because she was so used to him now. And she did wonder now and then if she wasn't losing out on something by restricting herself to one guy. But wouldn't she miss him terribly if she didn't see him at all? That was an awful thought, but she was startled to find herself thinking she might *not* miss him so much. Why did being in love have to be so complicated?

Pamela straightened up and stepped back hastily from the window. Jonathan's old Chevy convertible, Big Pink, was pulling up to the curb in front of the house. She contemplated telling Jonathan and Fiona that she wasn't feeling well and would have to skip the party. They would immediately guess her real reason for staying home, of course. How much fun could she have if she felt like the only one there who wasn't part of a couple?

Matt had already spoiled half of her weekend. Was she going to let him spoil the other half as well? That would be a really dumb move. It looked like a perfect day for the beach. Why should she waste it sitting at home moping? Everybody she knew — except Matt, of course — was going to be there, and a day of fun in the sun with friends would help take her mind off her problems. Besides, she knew about Laurie Bennington's fabulous parties, and she thought she would be an utter fool to pass one up just because Matt wasn't coming with her.

She rushed around her room, stuffing her tote bag to capacity with her bathing suit, cover-up, towel, shampoo, hair brush, and sketching materials. As she passed the hall closet on the way out the door she added a Peruvian shawl in case the weather turned cooler after sundown.

Someone was sitting in the backseat, behind Jonathan. As she neared the car, she was surprised to feel a rush of excitement when she realized it was her fellow counselor, Ben Forrest. He turned and waved and Pamela greeted him with a big smile.

"Ben had a sort of transportation crisis this morning," Jonathan said.

"That's Washingtonese for a car that won't start," Ben explained with a smile. "Besides, it was really two crises. Elise can't get away until later this afternoon, and it didn't make sense for us to take two cars, so I threw myself on Jonathan's mercy."

"You really ought to get Matt Jacobs to look at your car," Fiona said in her crisp English accent. "He's marvelous with automobiles, isn't he, Pamela?"

Pamela nodded.

"Good idea," Jonathan said. "Maybe you should call him at the gas station, and ask if he'll take a look at it when he's done this afternoon. We could even drive by on the way to Laurie's if you like."

"I don't think — " Pamela began, then stopped.

"We *are* running just a bit late," Fiona said diplomatically. "I'm sure a telephone call will do the trick quite as well as a visit."

Pamela gave her a grateful look.

As they drove off, Ben turned and said, "Are you all ready for the big day tomorrow?"

"Well, if I stop to think about it for more than five minutes I get butterflies in my stomach," Pamela replied with a grin. When Fiona looked at her curiously, she explained, "Ben and I are both going to be counselors at Camp Woodlands this summer."

"Are you? How lovely."

"We had orientation on Friday," Ben explained, "and Pamela was sketching the whole time. You should have seen the drawing she did of me."

Fiona looked thoughtful for a few moments, then said, "Have you ever tried sketching people for money?"

"No. Why?"

"Just wondered," Fiona replied, giving her a mysterious smile. Then, to Pamela's dismay, she turned the conversation back to Matt.

"What a pity Matt had to work today. Couldn't he have persuaded his uncle to give him a holiday?"

"Probably," Pamela replied, "but he didn't want to. He needs the money."

"He has to pay back his uncle for the loan on that incredible Mustang he found," Jonathan added. "I don't blame him. That has to be one of the greatest American models ever made. I'd work Sundays for one anytime, though my own dream machine is a Dodge R/T. Zero to sixty in six seconds!"

"Sounds impressive," Fiona said. "But as the speed limit is fifty-five, it can't be terribly practical, can it?" The look she gave Pamela said that they were fellow victims of Matt and Jonathan's mania about cars. Pamela rolled her eyes in agreement, but again she felt that same tingle of excitement she'd had when she climbed into the backseat beside Ben. What was the matter with her? Why didn't she care more that Matt wasn't there with her? She pushed the thoughts aside as she felt a shiver run up her spine when Ben's knee gently brushed against her own.

Half an hour before her guests were due to start arriving, Laurie took another walk around to check over her preparations. Everything in the kitchen looked ready. Outside, the men had set up the tables and chairs on the deck and lawn just the way she had wanted them. She strode across the lawn and looked down at the beach. The posts for the volleyball net were lying on the sand, ready for someone to volunteer to put them up. She looked up at the cloudless blue sky. It was going to be a very hot day. Maybe she ought to put a cooler of sodas down on the beach, handy to the volleyball court. That was the sort of touch that made her parties so great.

The only thing she could find in the storeroom

was an old Styrofoam cooler. She dusted it off carried it to the kitchen, and stacked a couple of dozen cans of soda in it, then added a bag of ice.

If she shaded the cooler from the sun and gave it another shot of ice in a couple of hours, she could probably manage to keep a supply of cool drinks down on the beach all afternoon. She returned to the storeroom and dragged out a big café umbrella.

Once she got it down on the beach, she couldn't get the umbrella to stand up. She tried to stick the pole in the sand, but because the umbrella was meant to fit into a table, it didn't have a pointed end. After the first few inches, she couldn't get it to go any farther. Still, it looked steady enough. She raised the umbrella and stepped back a few paces to study the effect. No question, it added a little extra class to the scene, a touch of European sophistication. It didn't look very stable, however, as it wobbled in the light breeze.

"Need a hand?"

Laurie looked up in surprise. It was her *Chariots of Fire* runner.

"Actually, I could use some help," she said. "I can't get this umbrella to stand up."

"Looks like you need some kind of base to support it," he said. "The sand won't do it." His voice was deep and strong.

"I guess not," she said with a laugh. She turned back toward the house, and he followed, carrying the umbrella. "I'm Laurie," she added.

"Rick. You live here?"

"Here and Rose Hill. How about you?"

"I'm from Baltimore, but I've got a summer job as a lifeguard down the beach."

By this time they had reached the steps leading up to the lawn. When he stopped, she said, "I'm throwing a party this afternoon. Why don't you drop by?"

He shook his head. "Sorry, I can't. I'm on duty. In fact, I'm late already."

"That's too bad." She gave him one of her famous long, penetrating looks, but she couldn't tell if he noticed. "How about after dinner?"

"Sorry," he repeated. He seemed to mean it. "See you on the beach, Laurie."

"Sure, Rick." As she watched him lope off, she wondered why she felt so disappointed. She knew nothing about him. Before she could ponder the question for long, she heard voices calling from the direction of the house. The first of her guests had arrived.

Chapter 8

The voice of Peter Lacey, Kennedy High's star D.J., boomed from the big speakers on either side of the deck.

"This one is for all of us departed seniors," he said. "And to all of you in the new senior class, don't forget: This is your time. Enjoy it while it lasts." As he spoke these words in an accent of doom, he blasted out the opening bars of Springsteen's *Glory Days.*

Woody Webster caught Peter's eye through the sliding doors and gave him a grin and a thumbs-up. Peter had a knack for picking the right music for any occasion. It usually turned out to be something by The Boss. He did play other music, the more obscure the better. It made his day to discover a new garage band from Tyler, Texas, or a tape by a Rod Stewart clone from Zurich who sang *Tonight's the Night* in a thick Swiss accent.

A hand clapped Woody on the shoulder and a familiar voice said, "Hey, how's it going?"

"Hey, Ted," he replied. "No complaints." Ted Mason was the former captain of the Kennedy football team and one of Woody's oldest and closest friends.

"Great party," Ted continued. They turned and looked over the scene in a comfortable silence. Eight or ten kids were crowded around one of the tables playing an intense round of Scruples. On the lawn, Chris Austin and her stepsister, Brenda, were leisurely tossing a Frisbee between them while an Irish setter that had joined the party from somewhere ran back and forth beside them, leaping and snapping at the flying disk. Four kids were playing badminton, and others were simply wandering around, sodas in hand, talking and enjoying the afternoon sun.

Ted glanced in the direction of a table loaded with chips, vegetables, and dips, and said, "What does Kim think of the food?"

Kim Barrie was Woody's girl friend of long standing. She had a professional interest in food — her mother was the owner of Earthly Delights, one of the most successful catering firms in the Washington area, and Kim often helped her out.

"She's not here," Woody said regretfully. "She and her mother are doing the opening of a new art gallery in Georgetown. This morning before I left, I had to help her arrange twenty dozen finger sandwiches in overlapping circles. They were supposed to look like flowers."

Ted gave a snort. "Is a finger sandwich anything like a knuckle sandwich?"

"Boor," Woody replied. "Peasant. Ignorant lout."

"I've been called worse," Ted said, straight-faced.

"Oh, yeah? Well, I could keep going," Woody replied. Ted stopped him with a not-so-playful punch on the arm. "Okay! Truce. Different subject — where's Molly?"

"Where do you think? If there's more than a cupful of water around somewhere, you can bet that she's swimming in it. See that dot out past the breakers? That's her. She found our East Coast winter pretty hard to take."

Woody stretched luxuriously. "Who doesn't? On days like this I dream of moving to the South Seas and living in a straw hut next to the surf. Of course," he added, "by now the straw huts are probably all twelve-story condos with balconies, but the weather must still be terrific."

"Yeah, but you just dream of it. Before she left California, Molly used to live like that. Outdoors all the time — at the beach, in the mountains, whatever. It's tough to give all that up."

Woody looked around at the beach and the water beyond. "She's not giving it up," he said, "just compressing it into fewer months. I bet when she was in California she didn't even appreciate days like this because she got so many of them. If you look at it that way, she's better off now than she was."

"Sure," Ted snorted. "And if she moved to the Arctic and got only one day of summer a year, she'd be in really great shape! Tell you what, pal — you stay here and philosophize. I'm going for a swim."

With that, he took off and went splashing into the waves.

Farther down the beach, Pamela walked along the edge of the water playing a game with the waves. As each one reached its highest point on the shore and began to retreat, she followed it down the wet sand as far as she dared, then followed the incoming wave back up toward the dry part of the beach. The goal was to stay just along the advancing edge of the next wave without having to run or dodge and without getting her feet wet. So far she was doing pretty well. But just as she was starting to feel complacent, a rogue wave surged up, much faster and stronger than its predecessors. Before she could react, the water was foaming around her ankles. The wave reached almost to her knees before it began to recede. She let out a halfhearted laugh and went to sit down on the beach.

She had left the party a short time ago because in spite of the light and playful mood, good food, and good friends, she hadn't been able to feel a part of it. Not without Matt. She reached out to pick up a shell and studied it through eyes blurred by a film of tears. She wasn't sure she would have felt a part of it even if Matt had been there. Lately she just couldn't enjoy herself with him, and that realization scared her. They had been going out for almost six months already, and after their shaky start, things had been almost perfect. So what had gone wrong? Why were there no more sparks?

She stood up and headed back toward Laurie's house. Maybe if she studied some of the couples there, she'd find some answers. Anyway, she was tired of brooding and feeling sorry for herself. It was time to have some fun.

As she neared Laurie's, she saw that about a half dozen of Laurie's guests were splashing around in the surf. Out beyond the breakers, someone was swimming parallel to shore with the strong, even strokes of an expert. She guessed that it must be Eric Shriver, captain of the school swim team, even before she noticed his girl friend, Katie Crawford, watching from a nearby dune. They were certainly a well-matched couple — Katie was a state-ranked gymnast and the leading spirit of the girls' gymnastics team at Kennedy.

Was that the reason Pamela and Matt were having problems? Were they simply too different? She was passionately involved with art, and he was just as passionately interested in cars, but why should that matter if they loved each other? Would they really make a better couple if she gave up painting and started learning about camshafts and piston rods? She'd never heard that you had to be a clone of the person you loved to make a relationship work. Why, that would be unbelievably boring. But wasn't she bored anyway?

She shook her head in confusion and continued up the beach toward the house. Someone had organized a lively volleyball game. As she was walking by, the ball sailed out of bounds and rolled past her feet. She picked it up and tossed it to the nearest player, Ben Forrest.

"Come on and join us," he called. "We're short one player. It's the juniors against the seniors."

"You mean the seniors against the has-beens," Diana Einerson said. "Sure, Pam, come play," she added. "We'll polish them off in no time."

From the other side of the net, her older brother, Bart, shouted, "Hey, Sis, are you going to serve or just stand around shooting the breeze?"

A ragged chorus of "Yeah, yeah, serve!" came from his teammates.

Impulsively, Pamela stepped into the vacant spot in the second line. The player next to her was Jonathan, who smiled and winked as he moved over. Diane's serve had just cleared the net and dropped almost at her brother's feet. Bart made a spectacular dive and managed to pop it into the air before he buried his face in the sand. His teammates' groans turned into cheers.

Phoebe Hall was in the front row. Red pigtails flying, she crouched and jumped up to spike the ball over the net, straight at Pamela. Her first thought was to dodge, but somehow her fists connected with the ball and sent it flying back toward the other side, where it passed untouched between Laurie and Woody and landed just within bounds.

"Nice shot," Ben said.

"Thanks," Pamela said, meeting his gaze. She meant to turn her attention back to the game, but she found it oddly difficult to take her eyes away from him. She noticed he seemed to be having the same peculiar difficulty.

A shout from behind her broke the spell, but even after she went back to watching the ball, her mind stayed fixed on Ben. What was he really like? He seemed sweet and a little, well, reserved. Shy, maybe. He was very different from Matt, that much was clear.

Again she felt that nagging thought that maybe she was limiting herself by going out with only one boy. What was there to make her think that another boy wouldn't really be better for her? She imagined herself and Ben as a couple. Well, it certainly wasn't a jarring image. In fact, she rather liked it.

"Pamela!"

She blushed and looked up. Woody had just served the ball high into the air and it was coming down straight toward her.

"Set up, set up," someone shouted from behind her.

For one instant she took her eye off the ball

and scanned the front line. Ben, at the far end, was watching her intently. When their eyes met, he winked at her.

In a rush of excitement, she refocused her attention on the ball and popped it up at just the right angle to send it in an easy lob straight to Ben.

It was a perfect set-up. Ben leaped up and spiked the ball over the net. Ted Mason jumped for it, but the ball had smacked the sand before he had half finished his swing. Pamela's classmates started cheering, and someone clapped her on the back. It was only then that she realized she had helped make the winning point of the game. Ben ran over and gave her an enthusiastic hug. The moment she turned to look in his eyes, he backed away with an apologetic murmur.

Pamela was excited and confused by Ben's behavior, but she wasn't about to try to figure it out now. She suddenly realized she was boiling from the sun and exertion. She pushed her hair back behind her ears and wiped the sweat from her forehead and cheeks. When Woody shouted, "Everybody into the water!" she was one of the first to react. The whole crew sprinted across the sand and hit the surf in a pack of ten feet across. The splash they sent up soaked even the timid souls at the water's edge.

After the first shock, the water didn't seem so cold. Pamela found herself waist-deep in the water, welcoming each wave as it washed past her. Then Brenda was standing next to her on one side, and Ben on the other, and Phoebe and Michael beyond him, and they were all holding hands like first-graders on a class trip and jumping up in time to the approaching breakers. Pamela threw her head back and gave a whoop of joy, and as the next wave neared the still-growing line, the rest of them shouted, too.

A gull that had circled down to study this strange ritual banked suddenly and flew off in alarm. Pamela noticed and laughed at its timidity. Then, gripping Brenda's and Ben's hands more tightly, she dove headlong into the oncoming wave.

The force of the wave tossed and tumbled her until she lost all sense of direction. Finally, just as she was beginning to panic, she found her footing and stood up. Immediately the ground moved violently under her feet, and she fell into the next wave. A strong hand grabbed her shoulder and pulled her upright again.

"Sorry," Ben said. "You were standing on my back. Are you okay?"

She nodded and pushed the wet hair out of her eyes, then glanced down at his hand, now resting gently on her bare shoulder. Ben turned bright red and jerked away. Pamela noticed the color spread down his neck and along his collarbones. Then she realized that she was staring, and she, too, turned pink.

Ben looked past her. "Here comes a big wave," he warned. He held out his hand. "Jump or dive through?"

"Jump!" She grabbed his hand just as the wave crested and broke right in front of them. The force of it knocked her feet from under her, and she fell with a gigantic splash, pulling Ben down half on top of her. He scrambled away almost frantically, then turned back to help her up.

The moment she was on her feet again, she let go of his hand. "Thanks," she said, not meeting his eye.

"That's all right."

A few yards away, Fiona, seated on Jonathan's shoulders, was grappling with Phoebe, on Michael's shoulders. Fiona looked over at Pamela and shouted, "Help!"

Pamela glanced at Ben, who shrugged and said, "We'll be the Camp Woodlands team, I guess."

"Hey, that's right." She felt relieved by the thought, though relieved of *what*, she wasn't sure. Ben knelt down until the water reached his chin, and she climbed onto his shoulders. When he straightened his legs, the water was miles and miles below her, and only his hands on her ankles kept her from toppling over. They were strong hands with a sure grip, but she didn't exactly feel safe up there. The next thing she knew, they were charging through the waves toward Phoebe and Michael, who whirled around to meet this new threat.

In an instant, Phoebe went toppling into the waves. Then Fiona and Jonathan were right behind them, and Pamela, too, slipped off Ben's shoulders, pulling him after her. They both came up sputtering and laughing, trying to catch their breaths. When Pamela looked up, Ben was staring at her in a way that made her shiver. He took her hand and led her silently out of the water.

Chapter 9

Under an amber afternoon sun dotted by wisps of feather white clouds, they climbed down to the rock-strewn beach below the camp grounds. Dick led the way, turning occasionally to help Roxanne and Frankie navigate their descent over the jagged rocks.

The beach was a narrow strip of dark brown sand and darker rocks, four or five yards at its widest. The foamy ocean waves hit hard against the rocky shore, making a constant roar that drowned out the shrill cries of swooping gulls. Above them, the yellow mansion jutted out over the cliffside and seemed to be peering down on them, a watchful Victorian mother.

"This is exciting," Roxanne said, smiling at Dick and squeezing his hand as he helped her over a slippery rock. Despite the chill of late afternoon, she wore pink short-shorts and a tiny pink halter top that didn't leave a whole lot to the imagination.

"So this is the rockbound coast of Maine," Frankie said, shouting to be heard over the crash of the waves. "Not much of a beach — is it?" Frankie was dressed a little more sensibly in jeans and a gray sweat shirt.

"You can thank glaciers for that," Dick said. He slipped on a wet rock and slid about three feet down the cliffside before catching himself on another rock. "Ouch. I guess I can thank glaciers for that, too!"

The girls laughed. "Isn't there a college somewhere called Slippery Rock?" Frankie asked.

Dick's answer was drowned out by the surf. Roxanne was ahead of them now, walking with long strides across the narrow beach, dodging the incoming waves that lapped close to her sandaled feet.

It didn't take much for either girl to notice that Dick couldn't take his eyes off Roxanne. With her strutting around in that skimpy outfit, who could blame him? Roxanne did have a perfect body. Walking across the beach, she looked as tall, shapely, and confident as a Miss Universe contestant — and she knew it.

They found a protected spot where the cliff formed a small pocket. The beach widened there, and the surf seemed a distant whisper. Dick spread out the olive green blanket he'd been carrying. Frankie put the picnic basket down and then dropped down beside it. Roxanne continued to explore, with Dick's eyes following her all the way.

"A couple of the campers are townies," Frankie said, trying to break the hypnotic spell that held him.

"Oh, really?" he said, not really hearing her.

Frankie went on anyway. She had decided that she was not going to feel awkward about tagging along on this little improvised beach party of Rox's. After all, Dick had invited her. And she could tell that Dick found her interesting, too.

"Yeah," she said. "A couple of kids I was talking to live in Staunton. It's the nearest town. Tiny, I guess. But it's a town. They told me the funniest thing."

Roxanne bent over to pick up a shell.

"Oh. Really?" Dick repeated, still staring like a hungry puppy at Roxanne.

"Hey — Dick!" Frankie waved her hand in front of his face. Finally, he turned to look at her.

"Oh. Hi," he said. "How are you?"

She laughed. "I was telling you about these local kids. Their fathers are lobster fishermen."

"Yeah. There are a lot of those around here," Dick said, actually looking at her.

"Well, they told me that every night their dads bring home lobster for dinner. Night after night — and they're *sick* of it; Can you imagine?"

"Poor kids," Dick said, laughing. "They'd probably kill for a hamburger, right?"

They both laughed.

He has the warmest laugh I've ever heard, Frankie thought, feeling a sudden pang of emotion, feeling herself falling for him, for his laugh, for his warm, open smile, for his dark, sensitive face.

What a lucky girl his girl friend is, she thought. And then watching Dick's eyes hungrily roam back to Roxanne, Frankie told herself, Maybe his girl friend isn't so lucky after all. . . .

"Oooh, that sea air is so refreshing," Roxanne gushed, dropping down close to Dick on the blanket. "Here — feel my skin. I've got goosebumps!"

She grabbed his hand and pressed his open palm against her bare shoulder. "You're soaking wet," he said, surprised. She removed his hand from her shoulder and smiled at him.

"Aren't you cold?" he asked, looking a little uncomfortable since she had chosen to sit so close to him.

"No, not me," she said softly, kittenishly. "I'm a very warm person."

"You'll catch your death," Frankie muttered from the other side of the blanket. Neither of them seemed to hear her.

I'm not going to feel awkward, Frankie told herself. I'm not going to let them make me feel awkward. But she had to admit. She felt terribly awkward. She never should have come.

"Frankie was telling me about some local kids she met," Dick told Roxanne, giving her the warm smile he had given Frankie a few minutes before.

"Oh, really," Roxanne answered, sounding bored. "I've got an idea, Dick. Let's go for a little expedition — you know, explore the cliffside a little."

"Okay. Good idea." Dick jumped to his feet. He was eager to move. Sitting so close to Roxanne like that was driving him crazy. He brushed some sand off his jeans and looked down at Frankie. "Wanna come with us?"

Standing behind Dick, Roxanne was giving very unsubtle signals that she didn't want Frankie's company on this expedition. "Uh . . . no. You go ahead," Frankie said, reaching into the picnic basket. "I brought some computer notes down with me. I want to get started on them. Go ahead. Really. See you later."

They had started walking away before Frankie finished talking. She cursed herself for being such an idiot. And such a sucker. The computer notes she took out to work on were for Roxanne.

"That's me," she told herself. "I'm Roxanne Easton's friend. And I guess that'll be my identity forever." She looked up in time to see Roxanne take Dick's hand in hers as they ambled slowly down the beach.

Chapter 10

Elise came to the end of *Curious George* and closed the book with a sigh.

"That's a funny book," Joelle said, looking up at Elise wide-eyed. "I like the part where he gets carried away by the balloons. Elise, could that really happen?"

Elise smiled at the tiny seven-year-old who would be having her tonsils out the very next day. "Of course not. It's just a story."

"Even if you're very small? George is very, *very* small."

"Not even then," Elise insisted. "There is a special kind of balloon that takes people up in the sky, but it's much bigger than the kind in the book. It's almost as big as a house. I'll bring you a picture of one tomorrow."

"That'd be nice," Joelle said. "I like balloons,

but I don't think I'd like to be carried off by one."

Elise made a mental note to bring Joelle a balloon the next day.

"I'll see you tomorrow, Joelle, okay?"

Joelle beamed. "Okay. Will you read me *Curious George* again?"

"Of course I will." Elise smiled at her small charge, then ran her fingers through Joelle's curly blonde hair. "See ya."

As she walked out of the room, she glanced at her watch. If she left soon, she could make it to Laurie's beach party before dark. It was a shame that she had had to miss so much of it, but the kids here needed her. There would be other parties.

Marcie, one of the newer volunteers, greeted her in the corridor. She looked near tears. "Elise, I really need some advice," she said. "I don't know what to do with Tiffany. Whenever I try to talk to her, she acts like I'm not even there. It's been three days now."

As they walked down the hall, Marcie told her a little of Tiffany's history. She was six years old. Her father was out of the country on business and her mother worked full-time in Washington. A few days before, she had been hit by a car. She had a concussion and two broken legs, but the doctors were expecting a full recovery. It would take time, though. According to the orthopedist, Tiffany was going to be in the hospital for at least two weeks.

When Elise walked in the door of the room, the

little girl looked up hopefully for a moment, then turned away so that all Elise saw was a mop of dark hair.

"Hi, Tiffany," Elise said. "Marcie wanted me to come meet you. How are you today?"

The girl ignored her. When Elise leaned over the bed to pat her shoulder, her whole body stiffened. She looked terrified.

Straightening up, Elise said, "Marcie and I come to the hospital to play games with the children and tell them stories and talk with them. Did you know that? We're not doctors or nurses. We're just people who like to be with children and help them have a better time. What games do you like to play?"

No answer.

She looked over at Marcie, who shrugged and shook her head.

"Do you like to play with blocks? Or dolls? Or cars? We can bring some toys in if you like."

Still no response. Elise stopped for a moment and tried to think. If they waited for Tiffany to decide to talk to them, they might be waiting a very long time. And meanwhile, the little girl was obviously very unhappy.

"If you don't feel like playing with toys just now, I bet you'd like to hear a nice story. Let me see — " She rummaged through her book bag, pulled out *Curious George*, and began to read.

Before long, Tiffany was propped up on her pillows, totally engrossed in the story.

* * *

A half hour later, Elise made her way to her car through the hospital parking lot. She still had plenty of time to get to Laurie's before supper. As she was pulling away from the curb, the engine hesitated and gave a sort of hiccup. She frowned. She didn't use the car that often — had something gone wrong already? After a moment, the car ran smoothly, and she forgot her concern.

She pulled up to a stop sign and looked cautiously in both directions, then pressed on the accelerator when she saw the way was clear. As the car gained speed, she thought she felt a tiny pause. Had she imagined it? She concentrated her attention on the sound of the engine, feeling the vibrations transmitted to her hands and feet through the steering wheel and floorboards. She couldn't detect anything out of the ordinary. The car seemed to be running just as it always did.

Reassured, she leaned back in her seat and loosened her grip on the wheel. A moment later, the car hesitated again, throwing her forward. She hadn't imagined *that*. The engine was running again, but it didn't sound so smooth now. In fact, it was downright ragged, constantly changing speeds and missing beats. Something was definitely wrong, and whatever it was, it was getting steadily worse.

The smartest thing to do would be to pull over to the curb, but when she tried, she discovered that the car was now much harder to steer. She pressed on the brake pedal. Nothing happened. She couldn't seem to move it at all. Close to panic, she put both feet on it and pushed with all her strength. With a piercing squeal, the car came to a dead halt, still partly blocking the traffic lane.

She turned off the ignition, switched on the emergency blinkers, and slumped down with her eyes closed. Finally her heart stopped pounding, and she could breathe without gulping for air. She sat up and checked her watch. Her mom and dad were out for the day, and Ben was off at Laurie's beach house, over an hour away. All she could do was walk to the intersection up ahead and look for help.

On foot, the distance was longer than it had looked from the car. When she finally reached the intersection, her heart sank. What she had thought was a shopping area was just a used car lot. No one was around. Down to the left, however, she saw what looked like a service station. With a sigh of relief, she headed in that direction. A truck drove past, braked noisily, and began to back up toward her. She gulped and looked hastily around. If she had to start running, which direction should she take?

The driver leaned out of the truck and said, "Hi. Elise?"

She looked up and relaxed a bit. It was Jonathan's friend Matt Jacobs. Was she ever glad to see him!

"You having trouble?" he continued. "Anything I can do?"

"I don't know. My car stopped." As she spoke, she read the letters on the door of the truck:

ROSE HILL SERVICE CENTER — TOWING — ROAD SERVICE. "Do you think you can help?"

"I can try," he said cheerfully. "Where is it?"

"About half a mile down that way."

"Are you out of gas?"

She hesitated. "I don't think so. . . ."

"Never mind, I'll pick up a gallon at the station on the way. Hop in." He pushed the door open and held it.

Before driving off, he looked over at her and smiled again. She couldn't help but smile back. He was very handsome, and he had an incredible smile.

She sat back in the seat, closed her eyes, and sighed deeply. What a summer this was turning out to be, when the most exciting thing that had happened was having her car break down. What was wrong with her life?

"Don't worry," Matt said. "Most of the time it's something very simple."

For one crazy moment she was sure that he had been reading her thoughts. Then she realized that he was talking about the car.

Five minutes later she was back in the driver's seat. From under the open hood, Matt said, "Give it a try." She turned the key. The engine seemed to start, then died immediately. He came around to her window, wiping his hands on an orange cloth.

"Well, you're not out of gas," he said.

She was fascinated by his rugged good looks and his gruff but soft-spoken manner. At first, upon seeing his biceps bulge out from under his rolled-up sleeves, she had thought he must be a jock who spent all his time pumping iron. But as she watched, she realized that his muscles came from use, from physical work. He didn't even seem to be aware that he had them, though he couldn't have done what he did without them.

She realized he was watching her face, waiting for a response. "Oh, good," she said vaguely. When he bent over and rested his elbows on the lowered door window, she could feel his breath on her face. She studied his warm eyes and full lips and felt a shudder run down the base of her spine.

"Uh-uh, not good. That means it's something else."

"Oh," Elise said, startled when he broke into her thoughts. "I don't know what my mom will say," she said, letting out a groan. "She had the car in the shop just a couple of weeks ago."

"She did? What for?"

"I don't know. Something needed fixing with the gas tank, I think."

"Aha. That just may be the answer." He vanished under the hood again. Elise got out to watch. He moved as if he knew exactly what he was doing and exactly how to do it. She got the same kind of feeling from watching him work on the engine that she did from watching someone like Katie go through a gymnastics routine. He moved in the same smooth, well-thought-out way. He was obviously good with his hands.

Good with his hands. . . . Maybe it was the phrase itself that made her wonder what it would be like to be in his arms. They were strong arms, but every move he made revealed their delicate precision, and there was a certain gracefulness to his movements as well. She tried to imagine what kissing him would feel like, and decided that behind a hint of gruffness, he would be incredibly gentle.

He lifted his head, met her eyes, and smiled. Her face was instantly flooded with warmth. She was irrationally sure that he had read her very thoughts once again. Stranger still, she was just as sure that his own thoughts had been a lot like hers. Not that it really mattered. He might be very attractive, and nice, too, but she was in love with Ben, wasn't she?

"Hey, okay!" He was grinning at her over the small cylindrical gizmo he was holding up. "Look at that!"

"Is that what caused the problem?" she asked incredulously. "What is it?"

"That's your gas filter, and it's totally clogged. Whoever worked on the gas tank must have stirred up a lot of rust and gunk. Once the filter clogged, the rust jammed the carb, too."

"Can you fix it?"

"Sure. Leave the car at the station, and

tomorrow I'll pull the gas tank and send it over to be boiled out."

"Mom'll just die," Elise wailed. "I'm sure she needs the car tomorrow. Isn't there any way — "

He frowned and rubbed the back of his neck. "I can talk to my uncle about giving you a loaner. We do that sometimes."

"Really? That would be great!" She beamed at him. To her surprise, he blushed. Then he vanished under the hood again.

Five minutes later he got behind the wheel and turned the key. The engine started with a roar. He revved it a few times, then climbed out and held the door for her. As she got in, she felt suddenly shy and self-conscious. He leaned down until his face was very close to hers. For a brief moment she was sure he was going to kiss her.

He straightened up with a jerky speed that was totally unlike the graceful movements she had seen earlier. "I'll follow you to the station," he said.

"Good idea. And Matt?" she paused. "Thanks a lot, really. You've been a life saver."

"No problem," he said awkwardly, then grinned. "Hey, did I tell you I saw you the other day?"

"No. Where?"

"Climbing up a ladder in front of a house on Everett Street."

She remembered now. It had been his car she had seen. How could she have gotten herself into such a ridiculous situation? She looked down at her feet in embarrassment.

"That's where I live," she mumbled. "I was locked out."

"Yeah, I figured that out." He laughed. "And anyway, I didn't believe someone so cute could be a burglar."

Chapter 11

"Over here! To me, to me!"

The big multicolored beach ball soared into the air and seemed to hover in the embrace of a fluffy white cloud. Then it plummeted downward. It was headed for a spot about two yards to Pamela's left. Knee-deep, she waded toward it against the constant resistance of the water. Michael Rifkin was coming from the other direction in leaping strides that looked spectacular and made a great deal of noise but didn't seem to get him to the target zone any quicker than her wading.

She dove forward, reaching for the ball, and managed to hit the surf belly first. She closed her mouth just in time, but she did get a noseful of salt water. She stood up, sputtering and coughing. When she pushed the dripping hair away from her eyes, she saw that Diana now had the ball and was trying to keep it out of Jonathan's hands.

It had all started when Jeremy produced a ball he had bought at the mall the night before. Blown up, it was fully two feet in diameter, but so light that he could easily throw it twenty feet into the air. A game of catch had turned into keep-away, and the first time the ball sailed into the water, they had all raced in after it.

"Shirts against skins," Woody had shouted. That got a laugh from everybody.

"You wish, Webster," Fiona had replied smartly.

Diana was twisting and dodging as best she could, but Jonathan nearly managed to knock the ball out of her hands. She made a quick, desperate toss, but Ben came shooting up out of the water like a submarine-launched missile and intercepted it. He held the ball high over his head and started running, raising his knees high with each step like a silent-film comedian. Brenda, Diana, and Phoebe all took off after him, while Jeremy and the other guys shouted encouragement.

"Watch out! Throw! Throw!"

The voice was practically in Pamela's ear. She glanced over her shoulder and saw Michael poised to catch Ben's pass.

"Over here, Ben!" he cried.

Michael started to move in front of her, then seemed to fall over his own feet. The next thing she knew, the ball was coming straight at her, very quickly. Pamela yelped, threw her hands up, and shut her eyes tightly.

When she opened them a moment later, she had the beach ball in her arms, and the other girls were cheering. Michael struggled to his feet and reached for it, but she passed it to Fiona. Fiona paused to stick out her tongue at the other team, then calmly tossed the ball into the make-shift goal box they had set up for the winning point. Ben dove for the ball but missed.

"Boo!" Jonathan called through cupped hands. "Boo! Fix!" He raised one hand to point at Ben. "Forrest took a dive," he continued loudly. "He threw the game!"

Ben just grinned, spread his arms wide like a gorilla, and started to wade in Jonathan's direction.

Jonathan slowly backed away, taunting Ben as he went, accusing him of deliberately tossing the ball to Pamela and letting the girls win. Pamela was about to protest when Ben crouched down and leaped at Jonathan, who stepped deftly aside and let him do a belly-flop. The splash caught Jonathan, but it also drenched Bart, who hadn't even been involved in the game. He spun around and sent a faceful of water at Ben, who had just surfaced and was still sputtering. As if on signal, every guy in a ten-foot radius was splashing water at everyone else, laughing like hyenas all the while.

As Pamela turned away, she met Phoebe's gaze. Phoebe rolled her eyes upward and fluttered her eyelids, as if to say, "Boys!" Pamela smiled in response, then noticed Jonathan and Ben heading toward her. She shot a big spray of water at Jonathan. He ducked, not very successfully, then used the side of his foot to send a wall of water in her direction.

Ben quickly came to her defense. Throwing himself in front of her, he began to attack Jonathan with a barrage of splashes. When Jonathan finally escaped, Ben turned around quickly, sending himself and Pamela tumbling into the waves. Practically choking she was laughing so hard, she reached for Ben's outstretched hand and let him pull her surely to her feet until she was wrapped in his arms. For a moment she rested her cheek against his shoulder. The feel of his hands resting so lightly on her back raised goosebumps on her arms, and she could feel her heart pounding. How natural it felt to stand close to someone like this. To someone . . . someone who *wasn't* Matt Jacobs.

She pressed her palms against Ben's chest and leaned back to look into his eyes. He looked back uncertainly and seemed as confused by their embrace as she was. He gave her a flickering half smile, inviting her to pretend with him that they were simply playing some sort of game. But they both knew better. Whatever was happening, wherever it might lead, this was obviously no game.

Laurie had planned the simplest supper menu

she could think of: hamburgers, hot dogs, potato chips, and a green salad. She hadn't been able to resist a few exotic touches, such as a dish of Indian mango chutney, a jar of French mustard with green peppercorns, and a bag of fried plaintain chips from the West Indies, but apart from that the meal was as American as any backyard cookout.

Now all Laurie needed was a couple of cooks. She took a look around her. Woody was showing off his virtually nonexistent muscles to Chris — whose long lithe body looked sleek in her pale blue one-piece — and Molly, whose compact shape radiated fitness. The girls were laughing at the stripes created by Woody's T-shirt sleeves. His shoulders were pale and his forearms had the beginnings of a sunburn.

"Why, Woody," Laurie cooed, "aren't you just dying to flex those muscles over a grill, deftly flipping burgers to feed this hungry horde?"

"Uh, how about we order a couple of Super Salami Sinker Subs instead?" Woody evaded, wiggling his bushy eyesbrows.

"Woody, the sub shop is an hour away — they'd be fried by the time they got here."

Just then, amid a chorus of "Yuck!" "Gross!" "Fried salami, blah!" Jeremy volunteered Fiona and Diana for positions as cooks. The girls protested violently.

"Hey, I think it's the guys' turn," Phoebe announced, tossing back her thick red pigtails. "After all, I can speak for the women around here — doing more than their share of cooking at our cabin in the mountains; right, boys?"

Ted, Bart, Woody, and Jeremy protested feebly. Woody suddenly developed a mysterious cramp in his shoulder, which prevented his lifting his arm to turn the hamburgers over. He collapsed on the sand. Everyone just rolled their eyes and laughed.

Fiona turned to Jeremy and said tartly, "Why don't you put up or shut up? I don't see you volunteering." But she gave him a mischievous grin to take the sting out of her tone.

Diana took up the challenge and turned to Bart. "What's your excuse, Mr. Einerson? I recall not a few cookouts back on the ranch during roundups when you cooked for a whole bunch more people, who were a lot hungrier, and not nearly as much fun as these guys!"

Laurie was enjoying herself immensely. The rest of the kids had gathered around. Pamela stood just a little apart from Ben, and Jonathan was watching Fiona with an amused grin.

"Okay, okay! We surrender," Bart said sheepishly. "Come on, Jeremy. We'll make them sorry they ever asked us to cook. Where's the hot sauce? Laurie, do you have any jalapeño peppers? This is going to be one cookout you Easterners are never going to forget!"

Jeremy turned to Bart in mock horror. "Some friend you are, drafting me! How about I pass up this chance and promise you all a fish-and-chips bash at our house next time?"

"Oh, no, you don't," Laurie said. "You'll probably trick Fiona into managing that one. To the grill, Jeremy, to the grill."

At that, Bart and Jeremy followed Laurie back up to the tables, where she had set up the hamburger patties and various toppings. Woody led the rest of them back to the beach, and a heated game of Frisbee started up.

Bart lit the charcoal and within half an hour, pronounced it ready. A few minutes later, the unmistakable aroma of hamburgers cooking on a charcoal grill was wafting out over the beach. Jeremy set up the chips and dip and opened fresh cans of ice-cold soda. A few minutes after that, people began to drift up from the beach and gather on the deck. They looked tired and happy, though judging by the shade of pink some of them had turned, they weren't going to be so happy by morning.

Pamela waited in line for her minute under the shower head at the side of the house, then went inside to towel off. She quickly changed into shorts and an oversize sweat shirt and went back out on the deck.

The chow line was already forming. She took her place behind a group that included Ted Mason, Molly Ramirez, Chris Austin, and Woody Webster. She still recalled how nervous she had been only a few months before when Brenda took her to the table in the cafeteria where these same people — the most popular kids at Kennedy High

— always sat at lunchtime. To her astonishment she had discovered that they were people just like anyone else, and most of them pretty nice people at that.

The games and the swim had given her a tremendous appetite, and as soon as Bart plopped a hamburger onto the bun she held out, Pamela brought her plate to the fixings table and began to convert it into what she had once been told was a California burger: lettuce, tomato, onion slice, pickles, and a combination of mustard, mayo, and ketchup. Out of curiosity, she added a spoonful of chutney before balancing the upper half of the bun on top.

From the far side of the deck, Fiona waved and pointed to an empty chair beside her. Pamela nodded and made her way over. Jonathan looked up and smiled, then returned to the serious business of demolishing what was left of his burger.

As she was about to take her first bite, something made her glance in the direction of the house. Ben was just stepping through the glass doors. His expression seemed a few degrees beyond thoughtful in the direction of worried. As he paused to look around, he met her gaze. When he started to head for her table, she found it hard to draw a deep breath.

He stopped right next to her, so close that if she had leaned only slightly to the right she would have been touching him, but he was looking at Jonathan. "Can you give me a ride home?" he asked.

"Sure. What's up?"

"Elise just called," he explained. "Her car flaked out on her, so she won't be able to get here."

"Too bad," Jonathan said.

"Is she all right?" asked Fiona. "Where is she?"

"That's the funny part. Apparently the car broke down just a couple of blocks from where your friend Matt Jacobs works. I told her she was pretty lucky. What if it had happened out on the highway somewhere?"

Pamela's stomach turned somersaults. What an odd coincidence. Here she had spent practically the whole afternoon with Ben, and Ben's girl friend had apparently been with Matt that same afternoon.

"I'd better get in line," Ben added, "while there are still a few hamburgers left."

"I'll join you," said Jonathan, wiping his hands on his napkin. "I'm about ready for another."

"I think the word *carnivore* was originally coined to describe Jonathan," Fiona said lightly as the two guys walked away. "Oh, there's Brenda. Do you suppose she has someone to sit with already?" She waved, and a moment later Brenda took the seat across the table and gave Pamela a warm smile.

"Hey, Fiona," Brenda said. "Have you told Pamela about your project yet? I bet she can be a lot of help with it."

"No, actually, I haven't. Jonathan and I were planning to make a general announcement after everyone is finished with supper. But it can't do any harm to get in a bit of practice, can it?"

She turned to Pamela. "We have a grand plan to mount an authentic old English Midsummer Revel in Rose Hill. Do you know *A Midsummer Night's Dream*?"

"I've never read it," Pamela admitted. "But I saw the ballet on TV last year. It was a little hard to follow."

"That must have been the Balanchine choreography," said Fiona, who had trained at one of the top ballet schools in London and was a professional caliber dancer. "Never mind. The general idea is that one celebrates the longest day of the year with dancing and merrymaking and such, because after midsummer, the year turns around and heads straight for winter."

"Brrr," Brenda said. "Who wants to think of winter in the middle of summer?"

"That's the whole point," contributed Jonathan, who had returned with a second hamburger and two hot dogs. "You enjoy a beautiful summer day a lot more if you keep in mind that it won't last forever. The thought makes you appreciate it more."

"When *is* Midsummer Day?" Pamela asked. "Sometime in the middle of July?"

Jonathan laughed. "That's the most confusing part. It's on June 21. It's really the first day of summer, not the middle. Please don't ask me why."

"It all has to do with the relationship of the

sun and the earth," Fiona explained, not very helpfully. "In any case, we've gotten permission to make use of the field at the top of the hill in Rosemont Park. It's quite a nice spot, with a lovely vista of the valley, and we're allowed to put up our maypole at the highest point in the park. That fits very nicely with the tradition."

Woody was walking by and overheard her. "Maypole?" he repeated. "I hate to be the one to tell you, Fiona, but you must have forgotten to tear a page off your calendar. It's June already."

"We know that," Jonathan said patiently.

"Maypoles weren't just for May celebrations," Fiona added. "In the old days they stood right in the center of the village all year around. There were different dances for each of the yearly festivals like May Day, Harvest Home, and so on. I know only a few, but I've a book at home that gives dozens of them."

"Count me out," said Woody. "Mister Two Left Feet, that's me."

"Oh, don't be so modest, Mr. Webster. I've seen you dance. And anyway, I'll only take people through the very easiest of dances, ones that even a three-year-old could do. It's really great fun, you'll see."

"It does sound like fun," Pamela said.

"We're planning to have a sort of parade at the beginning, too, with everyone in costume."

"That'll draw a crowd," Woody observed. "People love to dress up in costume."

"And then there's the traditional mummer's

play," Fiona continued, "all about the sun being reborn and growing strong, then starting to lose its strength. We were rather hoping Woody would take on putting that together." She smiled at him.

"With all your experience, you're a natural to do it," Jonathan added.

"With this short notice? Excuse me, I just noticed somebody I have to speak to." Woody started to edge away, but Jonathan grabbed the tail of his Hawaiian print shirt and held on. Woody looked down at the hand, then at Jonathan's face. "I'll give it careful consideration and get back to you. How's that?" Jonathan didn't let go. "Okay, okay," Woody said, "I'll do what I can."

"Super," Fiona said.

"I knew you'd see it our way," Jonathan added. "After all, it *is* for a good cause."

"It is?"

"Of course," said Fiona. "Didn't I mention that part? Any money that we raise will go toward restoring that charming old picnic pavilion in the park. It's in terrible shape. But everyone is going to have to help out. Without the support of every one of you, the first annual Rose Hill Midsummer Revel will be a washout."

Pamela glanced over her shoulder. From Fiona's tone and gestures, she expected to find a crowd gathered around listening. There was no one there.

Jonathan noticed her puzzlement. "She's practicing her speech for after dinner," he explained.

Chapter 12

The narrow strip of beach that Dick and Roxanne discovered ended at a large, prune-shaped black rock that jutted from the cliffside into the water. Dick peered up at the top of the rock. It was flat and smooth.

"Ooh, let's climb up and watch the sunset," Roxanne said, her voice even more whispery than usual. She was holding Dick's hand tightly.

"I'm afraid the sun sets in the *west*," Dick said, grinning.

Her lips formed that pout that just about drove him crazy. "Oh." She looked disappointed. "You know everything, don't you."

He put his hands on her waist and gave her a boost up onto the top of the rock. "Let's pretend we're watching the sunset," he said. He jumped up after her.

"It's beautiful here without a sunset," she said, lying down on her back on the flat rock, looking up at him.

"Yeah. I think the scenery is pretty terrific," he said. He gave her a sly wink. She already knew what scenery he was enjoying — and it wasn't the ocean or the beach.

She stretched her arms up over her head. "Oh, I feel so comfortable here," she said, smiling up at him. It was more than a comfortable smile; it was an inviting smile.

"Do you have a boyfriend?" he asked suddenly.

The question surprised her. Her smile faded for a second, but she quickly returned it. "Not at the moment," she said coyly.

This is it, she decided. I'd better make my move before he starts to tell me about his wonderful girl friend back home.

Dick was looking out at the water thoughtfully. He was probably thinking about his girl friend, Roxanne figured, beginning to question what he was doing out here on this rock with her.

Roxanne grabbed his shoulder and pulled herself up to a sitting position. When she was up, she didn't let go of his shoulders. Instead, she pulled him close.

She moved her hands to the back of his head, softly pulled his head close to hers, closer, closer, until their lips met. His lips tasted salty from the sea air. For a brief second, he tried to back away, to end the kiss. But then he held her close and began to kiss her as if he never wanted it to end.

"I'm very attracted to you," she whispered, her lips against his cheek.

"Me, too," he whispered back.

Laurie Bennington was a few hundred miles away. But to Dick, she was much farther away than that. She was gone, forgotten, completely out of his thoughts.

When darkness fell, Jeremy helped Laurie build a fire in a hollow of the dunes and everyone gathered around. Diana toasted marshmallows and passed them through the crowd, and Bart produced his guitar and started to strum. Soon everyone was asking for a favorite song. Bart did his best with requests that ranged from old camp favorites like "On Top of Old Smoky" and "Goodnight Irene" to "Jumping Jack Flash" and "Strawberry Fields." Peter Lacey asked for "Born to Run," but withdrew the suggestion when Bart told him he would have to sing it himself.

Gradually the mood around the fire grew pensive. Phoebe snuggled close to Michael and put her arm around his shoulders. When the tune Bart was playing came to an end, she began to sing an old lullaby, called "All Through the Night." A dozen voices joined in softly on the refrain, some of them in harmony.

Ben sat with his arms clasped around his knees, staring into the fire and thinking about Elise. Elise . . . and Pamela. He didn't understand what was happening to him. He missed Elise, he was sure of that, but how much did he miss her? It would have been nice to have her there next to him, his arm around her, and her head on his shoulder. But was that love, or simply closeness?

When you really loved someone, your heart beat faster when that someone walked into the room, and you wondered how you ever managed before you were in love. Ben remembered feeling that way about Elise a few months before, but not lately.

Whatever was happening, it was affecting her as much as it was him. Look at the way he had dreaded telling her how little time they were going to have together this summer. Sure, she had been angry at first, but she had gotten used to the idea pretty quickly, and she had never acted as if it made her sad. Was that the Elise who had been so crazy about him six months before? It didn't make any sense. But maybe love didn't make any sense.

Science was so much simpler. There were questions, and most questions had logical answers. And the answers didn't change on you in the middle of a problem.

Pamela was sitting halfway up the side of the dune, outside the circle, thinking about how the day would have gone if Matt had come to the party with her. She thought of how she would feel if she were staring into a romantic fire with the boy she loved by her side. Strangely enough, she didn't think she would have felt all that different.

She had had a wonderful day in spite of the fact that Matt hadn't been there. That thought made her nervous. But what made her even more nervous was the fact that she couldn't get Ben's image out of her mind. Visions from throughout the day kept flashing before her eyes — Ben next to her in the car, Ben on the volleyball court, Ben diving in the waves with her, Ben wrapping his arms around her. . . .

Why did she have this sense of dissatisfaction with Matt anyway? She wanted to feel a sense of excitement that brightened every day, made her glad to be alive, made her jump out of bed in the morning anxious to start the new day. She no longer felt the initial thrill that had been part of what she experienced when she first started going out with Matt, and she simply couldn't understand why.

Someone dropped down on the sand beside her. She glanced over, somehow knowing who she would see. The flickering light revealed Ben's face. He was staring down at the fire, but just as she was beginning to think that he didn't know she was there, he looked over and smiled at her. Her pulse gave a little jump.

"We'll probably be doing this a lot," he said softly.

For a moment she had no idea what he meant. Then she realized that he must be talking about camp. "I guess so," she replied. "I bet we'll be too busy taking care of our campers to enjoy it, though."

"That's a good reason to enjoy it as much as we can now."

"Yes," she said, in a voice barely above a whisper. She found herself leaning toward him, as if some mysterious force drew them together. When she felt his arm slip around her back, she rested her head in the hollow of his neck. Then his lips brushed gently against hers. She started to pull away, then as he began to murmur an apology, she held a finger to his lips to silence him. Reaching up, she wrapped her hands around his head and drew him to her.

Ben's kisses were sweet, a bit tentative, yet somehow wholehearted and earnest, completely different from Matt's kisses. But something about them felt so right. Pamela forced herself to abandon comparisons, pushed Matt from her mind, and gave herself up to the newness of their embrace.

At a little after nine, Jonathan came to find them. "Fiona and I are about ready to leave," he said. "She has an important rehearsal tomorrow morning and wants to get plenty of sleep tonight. If either of you wants to stay longer, I'll see if I can find you another ride."

"No, I'm ready." Pamela stood up slowly and stretched. "I'm starting a new job tomorrow morning."

"Me, too," Ben said, flashing her a knowing smile. "I'm ready, too."

"Let's go then. Fiona's up at the house getting her things."

Five or ten minutes into the drive back to Rose Hill, Pamela dozed off with her head on Ben's shoulder. When Fiona woke her with a gentle shake, they were just down the block from her house. She straightened up and yawned. An unfamiliar car was sitting at the curb just ahead of them.

Then she realized that the car wasn't *that* unfamiliar. It was the Mustang. She thanked Fiona and Jonathan for the ride, said good-night to Ben, and waited while they pulled away. Then she walked over to the battered convertible and knelt to look in the window. Matt had fallen asleep waiting for her. His face looked peaceful and strangely young, but there were dark patches under his eyes and lines of tiredness around his mouth. A wave of tenderness flowed through her. She wanted to wrap her arms around him and stroke his forehead while he slept.

Was it ESP that made him open his eyes? For a moment his face stayed blank, then he smiled at her, and her heart turned over in her chest.

"I must have fallen asleep," he said, sitting up and twisting his head from side to side.

"I could see that," she said with a smile. She opened the car door and slipped into the seat, ignoring the torn upholstery and broken springs.

"How was the party?"

"Not bad, but I missed you."

"I missed you, too. I came over the minute I got off work. I don't know why I thought you might be home so early."

"I would have left early if I could, but I was with Jonathan and Fiona." *And Ben*, she thought, with a tremor of guilt.

"I know." He met her eyes and held them for an endless time. Then he was holding her tightly in his arms, trailing his fingers lightly over the back of her neck. What's wrong with me? Pamela thought. Why does Matt's touch leave me cold?

Suddenly overcome with a sense of tremendous sadness and guilt, she pushed him away, jumped out of the car, and ran up the walk to the house. With her she carried the image of his baffled, hurt face. She owed him an apology and an explanation. But she couldn't apologize for being true to her own feelings. And how could she ever explain what she didn't understand herself?

Chapter 13

Every Monday afternoon, the high school volunteers at Children's Hospital met with members of the staff to share their experiences and talk over any problems that had come up. At the end of today's meeting, Virginia stood up to make an announcement.

"I know you'll all be happy to learn that Elise has agreed to help coordinate the volunteer program." She paused and cleared her throat. "One of her duties," Virginia continued, "will be to organize a training program for incoming volunteers. We'll also be developing an ongoing mutual support system, so that all our volunteers, new and old, know that there is somewhere to turn for advice, help, and encouragement. Elise, do you want to say a few words?"

Elise, taken completely by surprise, opened

and closed her mouth a few times. "Umm, just that I think what we're doing is incredibly important, and I'm proud to be working with such a great bunch of people," she stammered. "And anything I can do to make the program better, or to get more people involved in it, I will. That's all."

The others started to applaud, and Elise felt a surge of pride. They *were* a great bunch, and it was a privilege to be associated with them.

Marcie caught up to her as she was going out the door. "Are you busy now?" she asked.

"I was going to introduce myself to a couple of kids who just checked in today for surgery. Let me see — " She pulled the index cards from the pocket of her skirt. "Daniel is eleven and needs knee surgery, and Sharon is nine and due for an appendectomy. How's Tiffany doing?"

Marcie looked glum. "Same as the other day. I'll tell you, Elise, she's starting to get to me. After about ten minutes of her pretending I'm not there, I start to wonder if I really *am* there!"

"Hmmm. And I thought we were making progress the other day. Did you try acting as if everything were normal?"

"Uh-huh. I chatted about the weather; I told her a story; I even tried laying out the animal dominoes on her bed. She kept her head turned away the whole time. You know what scares me? I started wanting to reach over and shake her, just to get *some* kind of response from her."

Elise frowned and rubbed the back of her neck. "I wonder. . . . Have you had a chance to talk to her mom about the way she's been acting? Maybe she's just very shy."

Marcie shook her head. "I've never even seen Tiffany's mother. I asked the duty nurse about her, and she said she's here practically every night, but she doesn't even get here until after nine."

Elise reached a sudden decision. "Look, Marcie," she said, "how would you like to swap kids with me for a couple of days? You can look after Joelle, who's a sweetheart, and I'll see if I can't do something with Tiffany."

"I'm no quitter," Marcie said.

"Of course not. We're just changing tactics to see if we can get some forward motion, that's all. If I do get anywhere, we can switch again. Tiffany's going to be here for a while. And if I don't get anywhere, we ought to put her in the hands of one of the psychologists. She's a pretty unhappy little girl, and we have to do whatever we can for her."

After taking Marcie by to meet Joelle, Elise walked slowly down the hall toward Tiffany's room. Oddly enough, she found herself thinking about Matt Jacobs. He had been in her thoughts a lot since Saturday. She had been so impressed with the way Matt had gone about fixing her car. He had tried one possibility after another, and he didn't get discouraged when one of his ideas didn't work out. He seemed calmly confident that sooner or later he was going to find and solve the problem. The only question was how long it would take him. She could learn something from that. Right now she had two or three ideas about what the problem was with Tiffany. If none of them panned out, she was going to have to fight her feeling of discouragement and go on trying. It wouldn't be easy, but maybe it would help her to think of Matt, with his slow, sweet smile and strong hands — She shook her head and smiled to herself. Those weren't the sort of thoughts she had meant. Maybe it would be better not to think of him at all — if she could manage it.

Late that afternoon, Pamela was rinsing the last of the paintbrushes in the arts and crafts room at Camp Woodlands when she realized she was no longer alone. She turned to see Ben standing in the doorway. She swallowed hard and forced herself not to look away. It was the first time she'd seen him since Laurie's party. They had avoided each other on the bus that morning.

"Mind if I come in?" he asked.

"Of course not."

He stepped through the doorway, hands in his pockets, and looked curiously around the room. "How did it go today?"

She motioned with a paint-caked hand toward the back, where a couple of dozen sheets of newsprint were clipped to a clothesline to dry. He strolled over to take a look. Some were recognizably animals, cars, and faces, while others were more abstract. All of them, however, were blue. He studied them for a few moments, then came back.

"I like some of them a lot," he said. "But isn't there something a little, well, monotonous about them?"

Pamela laughed and told him she had only been able to find two kinds of paints in the storeroom. "I guess I could have admitted to the kids that we only have blue and green paint," she said. "But I figured if I did that, they would have felt deprived and unhappy. So I made it into a sort of contest. Today they had to see what they could do with just one color, and tomorrow they get to use two colors."

"Let me guess. Blue and green?"

"Got it first time. And by Wednesday I'll have the rest of the colors I need, even if I have to buy them with my own money. You know what? I kind of liked giving them only one color. I didn't have to keep telling them to put the red brush back in the red paint pot and the green brush back in the green paint pot!"

He wandered back to look over the day's production again while she washed her hands and scrubbed at her nails. "It looks as if most of them had fun," he remarked.

"I think they did," Pamela replied. "Maybe it came easier for them because they didn't have to make up their minds which color to use where."

She smiled at Ben. He looked almost as if he wanted to tell her something, but then smiled back.

"How was your afternoon?" Pamela asked at last.

"Pretty good. We went looking for trees that are either very tall or very wide, then we talked about why they grow in different kinds of places. Some of them made some very interesting observations that I never would have thought of."

"But isn't there one right answer?"

He gave his earlobe a couple of tugs, as if it were the starting handle for his brain, then said, "Isn't there one right way to paint a horse?" He pointed toward the clothesline. "Why didn't you just teach them how to do it?"

"That's different. Art is supposed to be subjective. Science isn't, though."

"No, but even in science there can be lots of different answers to a question, depending on what you want to know and what angle you look at it from. By the way, were two kids named Dave and Eliot in your class this afternoon?"

She groaned. "They sure were! How did you know?"

"I remembered noticing blue paint on their hands when they showed up for nature study. I have both of them in my morning group, too. They're nice kids, and bright, too, but you need to keep an eye on them all the time. They are the biggest natural cutups you'll ever meet."

"Please!" She craned her neck back to scan the

ceiling, then said, "Look up there. You see the blue marks on that rafter? Guess what they're from."

"That's easy. Blue poster paint. Eliot and Dave?" She nodded. "That must be eight or nine feet up," Ben remarked. "How could they — "

She rolled her eyes. "They decided to have a duel. With the brushes they had been painting with."

"Uh-oh."

"Uh-huh. It got pretty exciting around here for a few minutes. Then Eliot got lucky and sent Dave's sword — I mean his paintbrush — flying. The rafter was the first place it landed. The second place was on my shoe."

Ben laughed loudly and said, "I see how they got paint on their hands."

"Hands? You should have seen their hair. I wasn't super-gentle when I washed it, either. Maybe they'll be more careful next time. Hey, aren't we supposed to meet the buses back at the dining hall pretty soon?"

He checked his watch. "You're right. We'd better go."

As the two of them walked down the path, Pamela moved closer to Ben. She was glad there was no awkwardness between them after what had happened the night before. She had been a little worried when they hadn't spoken at all on the bus. But she had only wonderful memories of the time they had spent together.

Her thoughts must have somehow communicated themselves to Ben, for just then he glanced at her sideways with an odd expression. He took a step closer and held out his hand, palm upward. As she took his hand in hers, she wondered for a moment what the gesture meant. But after a brief squeeze, he let her hand go and slipped his arm around her waist. She knew what he meant by that. And as she let her head rest lightly on his shoulder, she knew what she meant, too.

Chapter 14

"There it is. The Staunton Diner. How quaint!" Roxanne exclaimed. She and Dick walked across the deserted main street of the tiny town. They stared into the window of the diner. It was filled by a giant fish tank, illuminated from behind with a bright green light.

"Do you think we have to pick our own dinner from the tank?" Roxanne asked, squeezing Dick's arm.

"I don't think so," Dick said, laughing. "These are tropical fish, Rox."

She laughed, too. "Wise guy," she whispered.

Suddenly his smile faded. "You know, we shouldn't be here," he said, looking up and down the dimly lit street. There were very few people out even though it was early evening, about seven o'clock. An old man was coming out of the General Store. A uniformed postman was locking up the small post office for the night.

"I know, I know," Roxanne said impatiently. "Town is off-limits except for certain nights. But no one is going to care if we 'break camp' just this once. Besides, what would they do to us? The whole camp only lasts two weeks."

I wasn't just thinking about that, Dick told himself as he stared into the glowing fish tank. He was thinking that he shouldn't be going out with Roxanne at all. He should be working on his computer project for the competition. And he should be writing to Laurie.

Laurie. He could feel his face growing red as she came into his mind. How little he had thought about her ever since he and Roxanne had kissed on that rock on the beach. For the past three or four days, he had been spending all of his time with her, neglecting his computer workshops, neglecting his project, and — in the worst way — neglecting Laurie.

He had even promised Roxanne that he would go out with her when they got back to Rose Hill. How could he have made such a promise? What could he have been thinking of? And what was he doing now, standing here in front of this quaint little diner in this quaint little town with this sexy, gorgeous girl who was anything *but* quaint?

"I don't like that thoughtful look on your face," Roxanne said, pouting. "You know, thinking gives you worry lines on your forehead. Here.

Let me help you stop all those troublesome thoughts."

She reached up on tiptoes and pressed her warm lips against his. When the kiss was ended, she stayed on tiptoes and looked into his eyes. "Did that work?"

He smiled and gazed back at her. "Sure did. I haven't a thought in my head."

"Good," she said, heels back on the ground. She pulled him to the door. "Now let's get some dinner."

The inside of the diner was as quaint as the outside. Faded fish nets were draped across the ceiling. An enormous lobster on a wooden plaque hung over the blazing fireplace, which cracked and popped, and gave a warm, orange glow to the tiny dining room. Black-and-white photo portraits of local fishermen in full fishing regalia covered one wall from floor to ceiling.

"Quaint," Roxanne said.

"Quaint," Dick repeated.

It was their buzz word for the night. Everything they saw, everything that came in or walked out of the diner was "quaint." And every time they said the word, they started to giggle, until after a while they were giggling without saying the word.

"Look at that guy in the booth over there," Roxanne said, pointing.

Embarrassed, Dick grabbed her finger. "Don't point. He'll see you."

"I'm sure he's used to being pointed at by tourists," she said. "He's so quaint." Giggling. "Don't you love that red-and-black-checked cap with the ear flaps! Why do you think he wears that in the summertime?"

"Never mind that," Dick said. "Why does he wear it in the restaurant?"

"I guess just to be quaint," she said. And they both laughed so hard, the waiter came over to see if they were okay.

Dick's expression turned serious. "You're thinking again," she accused him. "What about?"

"I was thinking about Frankie," he said. "She's working so hard. She seems to be working as hard as any two people in camp."

Roxanne decided to ignore that remark. She didn't want Dick to know that poor Frankie *was* working for two people — herself and Roxanne. "She's always been a grind," Roxanne said, shrugging.

Dick realized that Roxanne's green sweater matched her eyes exactly. He lost his train of thought, staring into her eyes for a while, then it came back to him. "She's very nice," he said, not quite sure why he wanted to talk about Frankie. "And very smart."

"Uh-huh," Roxanne replied, bored.

"You've been friends a long time?"

"Since fifth grade," she told him. "She was a grind back then, too. She's a lot prettier now, though. Her teeth got straightened, and she fixed up her hair."

The waiter brought their lobster rolls, and they dug into them hungrily. Someone started up the jukebox, and Waylon Jennings' voice suddenly filled the small room, accompanied by guitars and electric fiddles.

"What's your computer project for the competition about?" Dick asked, grabbing a handful of paper napkins from the dispenser to wipe his mouth.

"Uh . . . well . . . I'm not sure," Roxanne stammered. Frankie was doing the project for her, working very hard on it. Roxanne suddenly realized she hadn't even bothered to ask Frankie what the project was about!

"You haven't decided?" Dick looked surprised. "You'd better decide soon. We only have a few more days."

"What's yours about?" she asked, shouting over the country music.

"It's a program that a real estate office can use to keep track of its listings," he told her.

"Sorry I asked," she cracked, and pretended to yawn.

He gave her a hurt look. She grabbed his hand and squeezed it, smiling happily.

What am I doing here? he asked himself, feeling a sudden twinge of guilt as her hands closed over his. How can I let this happen after the promises I made to Laurie, after the way I felt about Laurie? I've been gone less than a week. Don't I have any more loyalty to someone I really care about than to just forget about her the moment she's out of the picture and start to —

His thoughts were interrupted by Roxanne giving his arm a hard squeeze. "Look — Dick — over at the table by the fish tank. Isn't that — "

He leaned forward in the booth so that he could see where Roxanne was pointing. "Yeah. It's the computer instructor from camp. Bill Willard."

Willard was slurping up a big bowl of New England clam chowder. He appeared to be alone at the table.

"Oh, boy. Now what do we do?" Dick asked, ducking back in the booth. "If he sees us — "

"Chill out," Roxanne laughed. "I think he's already seen us. What's the big deal? So we sneaked into town for dinner? It's not like he caught us actually skipping class or anything." She flashed him a devilish grin.

He was too worried to respond. "Let's get outta here," he pleaded.

"No way," she said. "He seems like a nice guy. He won't spoil our evening. I'm going over and say hi to him."

"Rox — " Dick tried to pull her back, but she was already out of the booth and walking over toward Willard's table, a big smile on her face.

Why is she doing this? he wondered. Why look for trouble? He watched her walk up to Willard, give him a foxy smile, put her hand teasingly on his shoulder.

Rox seems to enjoy stirring up trouble, Dick

realized. Look at her. She's flirting with him! And he loves it!

He watched them laugh about something she said. She put her hand on Willard's shoulder again. He seemed to like that, too. He wasn't a bad-looking guy, Dick decided. But he was too old for Roxanne. He was at least twenty-three!

Willard got up and, beaming from ear to ear, followed Roxanne back to the booth. "Hi, Dick," Willard said, reaching down to shake hands. "Night out, huh?"

"Uh . . . yeah . . . I guess," Dick said, unable to hide how uncomfortable he was. He was usually a straight-arrow guy. He seldom broke the rules. "We were . . . uh . . . just finishing," he stammered.

"Well, good," Willard said. "Pay the check and come along. I'll give you both a ride back to camp."

"Hey — thanks. That's really nice of you," Roxanne said, her whispery voice even more whispery than usual.

Dick tossed a twenty onto the table, and followed them out of the diner. The air was much colder than an hour before. He pulled his Windbreaker tighter.

Willard and Roxanne walked several yards ahead of him down the silent, deserted street. He heard Willard say, "Yes, I'm very impressed with your project so far, Roxanne. The groundwork looks good. I'll be interested to see what direction you take as you develop the program."

"Oh, thanks. I have a great project planned," Roxanne said with a smile.

That's odd, Dick thought. She just told me she hadn't decided yet what it was about. What's going on here?

Suddenly, Willard stopped walking and turned around to say something to Dick. "I'm a little concerned about your project, though, Dick. I really don't think you've been putting enough time in on it. This is supposed to be a concentrated effort, you know. Two weeks, over and out. You've got to really plug away at it. Know what I'm saying?"

"Yes. Thanks." Dick forced a smile.

Roxanne got into the front seat of the small Honda beside Willard. Dick was forced to squeeze into the back.

"You okay back there?" Willard asked.

"Yeah. Great," Dick muttered.

Just what I needed tonight, he thought to himself. A lecture. Well . . . maybe on second thought, I *did* need a lecture.

I haven't spent the time I had planned to on my project, Dick admitted silently. That's because I've been spending all my time with Roxanne. And spending all my thoughts on how guilty I feel because of Laurie.

Maybe I *did* need a lecture, a lecture about staying away from Roxanne.

But — can I do it?

Chapter 15

Laurie awoke early Wednesday morning overcome with a desire to take up running, which completely shocked her. She had a nagging suspicion it had something to do with Rick. She wasn't making any headway with him by merely watching him run by, so perhaps she should join him. On the other hand, she had never been particularly fond of exercise. Most days she did her twenty-minute celebrity workout in front of the TV, but that was purely practical. She believed in keeping herself in shape simply because she liked her body and the reactions it got. Twenty minutes a day was a small enough price to pay.

Serious exercise was another thing entirely. In commercials, the girls who were pumping iron or running a marathon were always perfectly made up and smiling like Miss America contestants.

She knew what they really looked like: hot and sweaty, with limp, lanky hair and faces that looked like something left over from Halloween.

Laurie knew hype when she heard it, and she wasn't taken in by it. When jocks started talking about the thrill of driving yourself to the limit — or beyond, she could feel her eyes glaze over. Some people could fool themselves into thinking *anything* was a thrill. Not her. The minute someone invented a pill or a machine to keep her stomach flat and firm, she would stop doing sit-ups forever.

Yet here she was at seven-thirty in the morning, rummaging through her drawers for running clothes. She had to try on several outfits before she put one together that felt right: a cropped purple sleeveless T-shirt, yellow shorts, a purple terry headband, and yellow running shoes with pale purple socks. Maybe no one would mistake her for the winner of the women's minimarathon, but they would certainly notice and remember her.

She let herself out onto the deck and did a few stretches. The air was tangy with the smell of the sea and still cool from the night. Clouds sailed the sky, creating patches of sunlight that moved purposefully across the water and the beach. One pool of light climbed the dunes to the house, flooding the deck with warmth. She narrowed her eyes against the sudden brightness. Should she go back for her Vuarnets? But before she could decide, the sunlight moved on.

At the head of the steps leading to the beach,

Laurie hesitated. Was this really such a terrific idea? Maybe she should have some breakfast first.

On the other hand, hadn't she always been warned not to swim right after a meal? That probably applied to running, too. The conclusion was obvious: Since she ought not to run before a meal or after a meal, there wasn't any time during the day when she *should* run!

Discovering no easy answer, she adjusted her sweatband to a more becoming angle, descended the stairs, and crossed the beach to the strip of firmer sand along the water's edge.

She set off at an easy pace, elbows high, breathing deeply and evenly, in through the nose for three steps, out through the mouth for five. For the first quarter-mile or so, as her muscles warmed up, she found herself enjoying the muffled impact of her feet on the sand and the touch of the breeze on her bare arms and legs. Soon, however, her left calf began to protest and threaten to cramp on her. Her right knee wasn't very happy, either, and she couldn't favor one without putting still more stress on the other. Her breaths were coming more quickly now, and she couldn't seem to take enough air in through her nose.

Did people actually do this for *fun*? It was hard to imagine. She slowed down, then stopped completely, and stood with her hands on her hips, panting and trying to recover her breath. She felt achy and cross, and she was sure that her hair was damp and stuck to her head like a helmet, headband or no headband. And of course that had to be the moment when Apollo, otherwise known as Rick, loped into view. He was gliding over the sand as if running were the easiest, most relaxing activity known to man. For one instant she disliked him intensely. But she smiled brightly anyway.

When he drew within ten feet of her, he slowed his pace and said, "Hi, Laurie. Out for a run?"

"Just a short one," she said modestly, as he stopped next to her, running lightly in place. "I'm a little out of condition."

He obviously wasn't. Judging by the sheen of his skin, he had been running hard for quite a while, but though she watched his chest carefully, he didn't seem to be out of breath at all. She, on the other hand, was still fighting back the desire to pant out loud.

"How was your party?"

"Stupendous. Everybody had a fabulous time." (Puff, puff.) "It's a shame you couldn't have dropped by at least for a few minutes." (Sigh.)

He grinned. "Yeah, but at least I sent someone in my place."

"You did? Who was that?"

"My old friend Rex." He turned his head and whistled. A red Irish setter galloped over the top of the dune, slid down to where they were standing, and started to lick his hand. "That *was* your Frisbee he came home with on Sunday, wasn't it?"

"I guess it must have been," Laurie said with a laugh. She stretched out her hand. "Hello, Rex. And how did you like my party?"

The dog sniffed her hand, then turned to look up at his master.

"She's okay, Rex."

The dog sniffed her hand again, gave it a couple of licks, and moved his head under it to be petted. As she stroked the soft fur, she felt a flush of pride, as if she had just been admitted to a select club.

"Your Frisbee's back at the house," Rick said. "It's got a few tooth marks on it."

"That's all right. Rex did beautifully. If he wanted to take a bite or two, I guess he was entitled."

She gave Rex a final pat, then straightened up and stretched in a way calculated to show her figure to its best advantage. To her secret delight, she saw Rick's bright blue eyes widen. He *was* aware of her, then. She hadn't been sure at all.

He started to bounce on his feet like a fighter shadowboxing, and she sensed that he was about to take off again. She quickly said, "Do you run every day?"

"Mmhm. Twice a day most of the time." He bent over straight-legged and touched his palms to the ground on the left of his feet, then on the right.

Just watching him do that made Laurie ache. She looked out across the water and said, "Wow. You must put in a lot of miles."

"I try to." He held his interlaced fingers to his chest, turned his hands palm-upward, and stretched toward the sky. His taut muscles flexed with the movement, and she decided he really was the most gorgeous guy she had ever seen. "I'm in training," he added.

Somehow she managed to resist the urge to run her fingers along his arms and over his chest. "Are you?" she said vaguely. "Terrific."

He tossed his head like a show horse entering the ring, and a thick lock of sunstreaked blond hair fell across his forehead. "Yeah. I'm planning to do a triathlon this fall. You can't do a triathlon without a lot of training."

"Of course you can't. What a silly idea." She wasn't about to admit she had no idea what a triathlon was. She stepped out on her right leg, bent her knee, brought her body down until it touched her thigh, and clasped her arms around her calf. This was one of her favorite stretches. It was great for the leg muscles. It also did a wonderful job of showing off the length of the leg that wasn't working.

Getting back upright wasn't that hard, but she wanted to do it in a graceful manner. At home, she usually just clambered up any old way. That wouldn't do now. Slowly, she straightened at the waist, holding her arms out for balance, then transferred her weight to the rear foot and pushed off with the other, as if recovering from a fencing lunge. An instant later she was standing upright, feet together, doing her best to look as if she did that sort of thing all the time.

He had certainly noticed. "Do you study martial arts?" he asked.

"Not really," she said in a self-deprecating voice. If her tone misled him, that wasn't her fault, was it? And anyway, she did have a videocassette at home of Bruce Lee in *Enter the Dragon*. "How about you?"

He gave a shrug. "I used to do tai kwan do, but that was before I got interested in the triathlon."

There was that word again. It sounded like something soldiers in ancient Greece used to throw at each other. She couldn't decide whether to go on acting hip to it and look it up when she got home, or confess her ignorance and let him tell her what it was. He already had her down as a devoted runner and karate expert; if she let his ideas get any further from reality, she might find herself making some very awkward explanations.

"Uh," she said, "the triathlon's quite an event, isn't it?" She hoped it *was* an event.

"Top of the heap," he said. "They might not have it in the Olympics yet, but for my money a triathlete is the best there is."

Well, that was no help, Laurie thought. This guy gave out information like a bank passing out free savings bonds. She smiled and gave an artificial laugh. "You may not believe this, but I'm not exactly sure how a triathlon works."

"Hey, that's okay," he said easily. "Lots of people have never even heard of it, it's such a new event. It's called a triathlon because it's got three parts, right? First you swim two miles, then you ride a bike fifty miles, then you run a twenty-six mile marathon. Some places they put the bike race first and the swim second, but the marathon's always last."

She stared. "You do all that on the same day?"

Her astonishment seemed to make his chest expand at least four inches. "One event right after another, without any breaks. The original triathlon, the one they run in Hawaii every year, is called the Iron Man."

"And do you do this every year?"

His chest shrank back to its original size, which was still pretty impressive. "Er, no," he said. "This will be my first one."

But now he was bouncing on his toes so vigorously that she was afraid he might blast off into orbit. "Well, I'm sure you'll do beautifully," Laurie said in a way obviously meant to flatter him.

"Really?" He beamed. "Yeah, I think you're right. But I have to keep the training going, that's the main thing. Which way are you headed?"

"Um, back to my place. But you go ahead. I'm not in your league."

"Hey, no problem. You set the pace and I'll follow. I've got another five or six miles to do this morning. A little break won't hurt me."

Laurie closed her eyes for a moment, hardly able to believe this was really happening. Things were going exactly as she had planned. She finally had a chance to get this Apollo where she wanted him.

"You ready, Laurie?"

"Sure, Rick," she said. "I was just meditating for a minute. I always do before running."

"Really? Martial arts stuff, huh? Some secret Oriental discipline? You'll have to tell me something about that. Maybe it'll help me in the triathlon."

Laurie took a deep breath and set off at the fastest pace she could manage. What had she gotten herself into?

Elise waved to the other kids in the room and sat down next to Tiffany's bed. Tiffany immediately turned her head away.

"Hi," Elise said in a cheerful voice. "I thought of you earlier today. I was looking for something in my dresser, and I came across this." She held up a faceted crystal that caught and fractured the light from the window. Tiffany's eyes drifted toward it for one moment, then she looked away again.

"Do you know what it is? It's a crystal. It looks like a diamond, doesn't it? I'm going to lend it to you for a few days. I'll fasten it to the window, and when the sun shines on it, it will make rainbows on the walls. Won't that be something to see?"

Tiffany still refused to look at her, but Elise went on chattering anyway. She rummaged in her bag and pulled at the book she had brought especially for the stubborn little dark-haired girl.

"I brought a new story to read to you today,"

she said. "Maybe you've heard it before. It's called *Sylvester and the Magic Pebble.*" She began to read the tale of a little donkey who found a magic pebble and accidentally turned himself into a rock. Before long she was as caught up in the story as ever. But she was not too involved to notice that Tiffany's body had stiffened when she came to the part about Sylvester's parents and their grief. Though her head was still turned away, the child was certainly listening.

When she came to the end and closed the book, a small voice said, "His mommy and daddy were very sad, weren't they?"

Tiffany's clear blue eyes were fixed on Elise's face.

"Yes, they were," Elise said carefully, "when they thought they had lost him. And they were very happy when they found him again."

"Sylvester was very sad, too. He wanted to be with his mommy and daddy."

"That's right. But he couldn't be with them because an accident had turned him into a rock."

"But then his mommy and daddy helped him get to be himself again, right? So he didn't have to stay a rock forever and ever."

"That's right," Elise answered. She closed her eyes for a moment and hoped she would find just the right words. "Mommies and daddies are very sad when bad things happen to their children. And they do everything they can to help their children get better again. But sometimes their children don't know that. They feel like no one is helping them and they won't get better, and that makes them very sad."

Tiffany nodded thoughtfully. "You know what?" she said. "I had an accident, too, like Sylvester."

"I know. It must have been very scary."

"Uh-huh. But you know what else? I got turned into a rock, too, just like Sylvester!" She reached down and rapped on her casts, then started to laugh. But as she laughed, her eyes filled, and suddenly she cried, "I don't want to be a rock! I want my mommy to make it better *right now*!"

Elise reached for the girl's hand and held it as she began to sob and call for her mother. When she quieted down, Elise said, "Did you know that your mommy comes here and takes care of you every night after you go to sleep?"

Tiffany shook her head warily.

"Well, she does. You can ask the nurse. You can even ask the nurse to tell your mommy to wake you up next time she comes."

"I want her here now."

"Sure you do. But you know your mommy has to work. That's why she brought you here to the hospital, where there are doctors and nurses to take care of you when she can't. Bringing you here is one of the ways she's helping you to get better. But you have to help, too."

"How?"

"Oh, by thinking of all the fun things you'll do when you go home, and by finding interesting things to do while you still have to be in the hospital. I can help you find things to do if you like, and so can Marcie."

For a few moments the little girl was so quiet that Elise wondered if she had fallen asleep. But then she looked up and said, "I want you to do something."

"Sure, Tiffany. What?"

"Read to me about Sylvester again. And this time I want to look at the pictures."

Later, Elise found her way to the hospital cafeteria and bought a cup of herb tea. Her plan to help Tiffany had worked far better than she had expected, but it had been a real strain. It made her think of the time their neighbor's battery had gone dead, and Elise's dad had given him a jump start. They got the neighbor's car started, but it drained her dad's battery so much that he could barely get his own car started. That was how she felt now — drained.

It was funny how she kept thinking about cars and problems with cars and people who helped solve problems with cars. Well, one person in particular. Matt Jacobs. He had certainly helped her when she needed it, but now she felt as if she needed a different kind of help that he couldn't give her. How could he? He was part of the problem!

She couldn't remember ever feeling so confused about her own feelings. She had still been up when Ben got home from Laurie's party on Sunday. He had seen her light and tossed gravel at her window screen. She hadn't really even felt like seeing him then. She was still so confused about her reaction to Matt earlier that day. When she did go downstairs to open the door, he hadn't acted like he had wanted to see her, either. He had told her briefly about the party, kissed her good-night sweetly, and promised to call her soon.

By Wednesday night, she still hadn't heard from Ben. But she had heard from Matt twice since Sunday. They were business calls, of course, at least on the surface. He had wanted to keep her up-to-date on the car repairs and to offer her a lift to wherever she needed to go while her car was in the garage.

She couldn't help wondering if the station's other customers got the same kind of personal attention. But when she pictured the way Matt had looked while he was working on her engine, she found that she didn't really care about the service station's other customers, or any of the other employees. Matt was a different story, though. She was thinking about him much too much. And she was beginning to sense that her life was about to become very, *very* complicated.

Chapter 16

When Jeremy came downstairs on Saturday morning, Fiona was standing in the kitchen eating a bowl of cereal and watching the Muppets on TV. Her left foot was flat on the gray tile floor and her right foot was resting on the countertop with her leg parallel to the floor. She stood this way a lot. She claimed that it was relaxing, as well as good for her extension, but then she had been seriously studying ballet for practically her entire life. The positions she bent her body into without even noticing would have put most people in bed for a week.

Jeremy walked across the room to investigate the contents of the refrigerator. Under one arm he was carrying an odd device that looked like a cross between an air rifle and a chrome bicycle pump.

Fiona glanced away from the TV and looked over at her brother.

"What on earth is that you're carrying?"

He paused in the middle of pouring a bowl of cereal. "Hmm? Oh, it's called a shotgun microphone. Very sensitive, very narrow focus. It picks up direct sounds and screens out background noise. You point it like a shotgun. That's how it got its name."

"Oh. Like a telescope, but for sound."

"It's rather like a telescope, or a telephoto lens on a camera. Actually, the chap I borrowed it from is an enthusiastic bird-watcher. He uses it to record the songs of birds on high branches."

Fiona put down her empty cereal bowl and leaned forward to grasp the toes of her right foot, the one on the counter, in both hands. She leaned over and rested her forehead on her leg just below the knee.

"What are you going to be doing with that shotgun thing? Eavesdropping on people's conversations?"

He poured a glass of juice and carried it along with his cereal bowl to the breakfast table. "Something like that, yes," he replied. "Actually, I got it with your Midsummer Revel in mind. For maypole dancing, the music is just as vital as the image, isn't it? The camcorder has its own microphone, of course, but if I'm shooting anything more than a few feet away, it's of less than no use at all. With this I'll be able to zoom the sound in as effectively as I do the picture."

"You *will* tape it, then?" She beamed at him. "Super!"

He smiled sardonically. "Well, after all, Fee, you did promise me all sorts of lavish bribes, didn't you?"

"Only a few," she said cautiously. "And I don't recall them as being so terribly lavish."

There was a tap on the door, and Jonathan stuck his head in. "Hello, Fee," he said. "Hi, Jeremy."

Fiona looked dismayed. "Oh, no," she said, "I'm not *nearly* ready. Excuse me." She ran out of the room.

"Hi, Jonathan," Jeremy said. "She'll be down in a minute. Have some juice. Off on an excursion, are you?"

"Yes. We're going up to Deer Pond Park for the day with Matt and Pamela," he replied. "It's a great day for it."

"Really? Diana just told me that we're going to meet Dee Patterson and Marc Harrison at Deer Pond Park for lunch and a swim." He glanced sidelong at Jonathan and added, "I can call her back and change things if that's too close for comfort."

"Not a chance, old bean." Jonathan seemed to get a kick out of speaking to Jeremy in what he imagined was authentic English slang. Jeremy hadn't yet had the heart to tell him that saying "old bean" to an Englishman was like calling an American "pardner."

"You won't be in our way, if that's what's worrying you," Jonathan continued. "We can even have an impromptu party. And if anyone wants privacy, it's a big park."

Fiona reentered the room, and Jonathan's eyes widened appreciatively. She was wearing a Laura Ashley sundress in a pale pastel floral print and a wide-brim straw hat with a band in the same floral print, which trailed down her back.

"Hey," he said enthusiastically, "you look as pretty as a picture."

"Page thirty-two in the summer catalog," Jeremy said under his breath. In a more audible voice, he added, "Are you sure that's quite the thing for sitting on the ground and eating hot dogs?"

Fiona stuck her tongue out at him and replied, "If you must know, I've got jeans and a jersey in my carryall. Now stop acting like my overprotective big brother."

"But I *am* your overprotective big brother."

Jonathan went to the door and began to fidget with the knob. "Come on, Fee," he said. "We're running late. I told Pam we'd pick her up at ten, and it's already ten after. See you later, Jeremy."

The door slammed behind them, and Jeremy drank the last of his juice and carried his dishes to the sink.

Pamela sat on the porch steps and tried to get excited about the picnic she had planned for that afternoon. She was going to have a relaxing, fun day at the lake with the boy she loved and their two best friends. Why didn't she feel better about it?

She wrapped her arms around her knees. Had it really been only a week since she and Matt had gone on that last disastrous picnic? It seemed almost to have taken place in a different lifetime. So much had happened since then. Those few minutes in Matt's car when she came home from Laurie's party on Sunday had haunted her ever since. She had been tired, of course. It had been a long day and emotionally very wearing. That must have been why she couldn't respond to him. And maybe she had still felt resentful over his decision to send her to the party alone. Maybe her coolness had been a way of punishing him. Then a few days later she realized that she hadn't spoken to Matt in three days, and she hadn't even cared. That spooked her. Was their relationship coming to an end?

She rested her cheek against her knee for a moment, then sat up, squared her shoulders, and leaned back against the step. Now wasn't the time to think about such things. It was a beautiful summer day, she was going to be spending it in a beautiful spot with good friends, and she and Matt would rediscover their delight in each other's company.

She heard a faint beep, and looked up to see Jonathan's convertible at the curb. As she walked across the lawn, a sense of déjà vu assailed her. She could almost imagine that she saw Ben sitting in the backseat, just as he had been on Sunday, but of course when she climbed in, the seat was empty. She slid to the far side and sat back, then met Fiona's gaze.

"Hi," Pamela said. "I love your dress."

"Isn't it super? I got it the last time I was in

London. There's a hat that goes with it, too." She picked the straw hat up off her lap and held it on the back of her head for a moment. "Smashing, isn't it?"

"Beautiful."

At the next traffic light, Jonathan said, "How about putting the top down?"

"Fine with me," Pamela said.

Jonathan flipped the latches that fastened the top to the windshield and soon they were driving fast, with the wind whipping their hair. Before long they came to Matt's house.

As Matt vaulted into the backseat, not bothering with the door, he flashed Pamela a huge smile that practically made her melt. Then he leaned forward and put one hand on Jonathan's shoulder and the other on Fiona's. Turning back to Pamela, he put his arms around her. The kiss she gave him lasted until the driver of the car behind them began to honk derisively.

During the drive to Deer Pond Park, it was impossible to talk over the noise of the wind, but Pamela didn't mind. She had so much to think about. What could she have said to Matt, or he to her, that said more than their embrace had said? And yet, in his arms she had felt warm and tender and close, but she longed to feel deeply stirred, and she hadn't. Was something wrong with her? Was she expecting too much? She fought to push the nagging thoughts out of her mind so she could enjoy the afternoon, but somehow she couldn't shake her dark thoughts.

Chapter 17

The narrow road into the park crossed a small stream on a wooden bridge that thundered under their wheels, then wound through dense woods that thinned out as it approached the pond. They began to pass parked cars and see groups of people near the picnic tables that were scattered along the shore of the pond. A tang in the air told them that someone already had a fire going.

Jonathan drove more slowly still. "Should I grab the first decent spot I see," he asked, "or keep going? I say keep going."

"The swimming beach is still halfway around the pond," Fiona observed. "Let's try to get closer if we can."

"Two votes for the beach. Pamela?"

She had been watching the way the light that reflected from the pond glimmered through the trees and lit the undersides of the leaves. It seemed to give even the air itself a faintly greenish hue, as if the woods, and they, were underwater.

"Oh, sure. Let's be near the beach if we can."

"The beach it is," Jonathan said, picking up speed. Suddenly the car swerved abruptly and stopped on the shoulder of the road just behind another car. On the rear window of the other car was a decal of a red bird with a red flower in its beak and the legend KENNEDY CARDINALS.

"Isn't that Michael's car?" Fiona asked.

Pamela stood up. That was one of the things she loved about a convertible, the freedom to stand up. "Look at the bumper," she said. "It must be Michael Rifkin."

The sticker on the bumper read MUSICIANS MEASURE THEIR TIME IN BARS and was decorated with a G-clef and a cello.

"It is Michael's," Fiona said. "There's Phoebe over by the pond. Shall we ask if they'd prefer to have privacy?"

"Sure," Jonathan said. "I'll go find out, okay?"

This turned out to be unnecessary. Phoebe had noticed their car and was coming over to investigate. She recognized them and waved. When she reached them, she was laughing.

"I was afraid you were trying to lift Michael's cassette deck," she explained. "He spent a fortune on it, and now he can't leave the car anywhere without worrying about it constantly."

"He ought to get — " Jonathan began.

"I know," Phoebe said quickly, lowering her

voice. "I'm planning to buy him an alarm system for his birthday. Hey, do you guys want to join us? We're a little low on drinks, but we've got three boxes of chocolate chip cookies. Michael is doing a research project to find out which brand he likes best."

"Great," said Jonathan. "We can help out with the research. And I've got a couple of dozen sodas in the cooler in the trunk."

By lunchtime, half a dozen more kids from Kennedy had driven by, seen their cars, and joined them. It was becoming a real party. Pamela went for a swim with Phoebe and Fiona while Jeremy, Jonathan, and Matt tossed a Frisbee around.

After lunch Fiona and Jonathan asked Pamela and Matt to take a walk around the pond with them. As they walked, Fiona and Jonathan gradually fell farther and farther behind, leaving Pamela alone with Matt for the first time in almost a week. She moved closer to him and put her arm around his waist. After an almost undetectable hesitation, he did the same.

After walking a while in silence, Pamela began to wish that Matt would say something. She hadn't seen him in days, and he hadn't asked her once how her job was going. That didn't seem right. It wasn't just that she wanted his encouragement and support. It was more basic than that. Being intimate with someone meant really knowing that person in a deep way. If Matt didn't know what was happening in her life and how she was reacting to it, how could he really know *her*? And it went the other way, too. She was just as much in the dark about what had been going on with him since school had let out. She felt herself losing touch with who he was. She decided to set an example by filling him in on some of the events of her past week.

"I don't know what to do," she began. "Eliot and Dave are getting to be a real problem. They show up almost every day for art class, but they won't do anything I ask them. If they'd go off in the corner and leave the rest of us alone, I wouldn't mind so much, but they disturb the whole class and they don't do any artwork."

"Eliot and Dave?" he said tonelessly. "Who are they?"

"I told you about them. *You* know — they're the ones who had the duel with paintbrushes the first day. I even showed — " She stopped herself just before she made a fool of herself. She hadn't told Matt about them or shown him their paintings. It was Ben she had talked to about Eliot and Dave, and Ben who had been constantly in her thoughts all morning. But the arm around her waist was *not* Ben's, not this time. What was happening to her?

Matt didn't seem to notice her slip. "If they don't behave, tell them to go away and not come back," he said idly.

She talked quickly, to hide her confusion. "Believe me, I've been tempted! But they're not mean or nasty, just high-spirited. I keep thinking that if I can only break through to them, I can give them a lot. They're in Ben's group in the morning, and he feels the same way about them. I'd ask Frank for advice, but I don't want to admit that I'm having problems this early in the job. What Ben thinks is that we ought — Matt, you're not listening. Is something wrong?"

He had stopped walking and was busy massaging the back of his neck. "Wrong?" he repeated. "No, nothing's wrong. I'm just tired, that's all."

"Tired? Or bored? I'm sorry if you don't find this interesting."

"Look, I'm having a problem following what you're talking about. I don't know who any of those people are."

"You know Ben."

"Yeah, but that doesn't mean I want to hear about him all the time. Look, we'd better turn back," he continued. "Jonathan might want to leave soon, and we don't want to hold him up."

Pamela couldn't believe the way he was behaving. His hostility felt like a slap in the face. She wanted to take him by the shoulders and shake some sense into him. Had he forgotten she was the girl he was supposed to be in love with?

"Sure," she said coldly, "let's turn back. I don't think the way we're headed is going to get us anywhere."

Chapter 18

The computer lab was dark except for the green glow of Roxanne's and Dick's monitors. The only sound was the click-click-click of Dick's fingers on the keyboard. Roxanne stared at her blank screen and sighed.

"I really don't understand you, Dick," she said. She lowered her lips into a pout. A few days before, he had said that her pouting expression nearly drove him crazy. Now he didn't even look up.

"Really, Dick. You can't treat me this way," Roxanne said, hating herself for whining like that. "You can't just — "

Bill Willard, the instructor, poked his head into the nearly empty lab. "Hey — ten more minutes, you two. That's all. I gotta lock up — okay?"

"Okay," they both said in unison.

"How's it goin'?" Willard asked.

"Fine. Just peachy," Roxanne muttered cheerlessly. Dick didn't bother to answer. He just kept typing away, his eyes reflecting the green glow of the monitor.

They heard Willard's footsteps recede down the hall. "So?" Roxanne asked, as if she'd been waiting for an answer.

"Please, Rox," Dick pleaded. "Tomorrow is the last day of camp, the last day to turn in our projects. I want to finish mine now. I just have a minute or two to go on it. Let me finish up, okay?"

"And then we'll take a walk to the beach, just you and me?" she asked, sounding kittenish again.

"No. Really I can't, Rox. Try to understand." He stopped typing for a second and gave her a look of regret.

"Understand what?" she snapped angrily, forgetting about her kittenish voice. "How am I supposed to understand that you've been refusing to see me or go anywhere with me for the past three days?"

"Rox, really, I — "

"How am I supposed to understand?" she continued, growing angrier with every word. "You are too busy to go to the beach, too busy to take a late-night, romantic walk in the woods, too busy to do *anything* with me! You've been completely ignoring me ever since we had dinner at that diner in town. So what should I understand from that?"

She slammed her hand angrily on the monitor top. "Owww!"

"Rox, I'm sorry. Really. I just — "

"What is this, Dick? Some kind of brush-off?" She refused to let him get a word in. He tossed his hands in the air in frustration and turned back to his keyboard.

"Don't turn around, Dick," she said, reaching over, grabbing his shoulder, and spinning him around. "Don't try to avoid what I'm saying. Is this a brush-off or not? I can't believe you'd do that to me. You know how much I care about you. And you said you cared about me, too. You do remember that, don't you?"

"Yes, but — "

"You even said we'd go out together when we got back to Rose Hill."

She tried to manage some tears, but they just wouldn't come. Instead, she turned her head away and shook her shoulders, hoping he'd think she was crying.

"Rox, I'm so sorry," Dick said with real feeling. He wasn't the kind of guy who liked to hurt people. He couldn't stand to see her crying like that. But he knew he had made the right decision. At least, he thought he had.

"I wasn't thinking clearly when I said that to you," he said softly. "I — I'm going with someone else. I told you that. I — "

"You said you'd break up with her," Roxanne said, trying to sound as if she were sobbing, and doing a very good job of it.

"I didn't mean to hurt you or anything," he said, his voice unsteady. "I was just so attracted to you, I guess I got carried away and promised things I shouldn't have."

The silence of the big, empty room enveloped them. He watched her back as she cried without making a sound. Maybe I'm making a big mistake, he thought. Look how upset she is, how much she cares about me. Maybe I shouldn't be throwing it away like this.

As she pretended to cry, her anger swelled up like a balloon, until she felt ready to burst. How dare he dump me like this? she asked herself, hardly able to control her fury. *I'm* the one who does the dumping! He has no right to reject me before I reject him!

This had never happened to Roxanne before. Her fabulous looks and her kittenish ways had always gotten her any boy she wanted. She had always been able to mesmerize them, to hypnotize them, to keep them as long as she wanted, until it was time to move on to the next conquest.

Dick's bizarre behavior, his sudden coldness after they were getting along so well, came as a shock to her. It didn't weaken her confidence in her ability to wrap boys around her little finger. It just made her furious.

Now she was determined not to let him get away with this.

She heard the click-click-click of his typing again. A minute later, his hand was on her shoulder. She turned to look at him. She had carefully smeared her eye makeup so that it would look as if she'd been crying.

"Listen," he said quietly, "I'm sorry. But I've gotta go. I think it would be better for you if I got out of here."

She didn't respond, so he continued. "Look, I just finished my project. I know this is a bad time to ask a favor. But when Willard comes back to close up, would you hand it in to him, please? Thanks, Rox. I'm going for a long run by the edge of the woods. That usually helps to clear my head."

I'll help you clear your head, she thought. With a baseball bat!

But she looked up at him with a mournful expression and whispered, "Can I come, too?"

"Sorry," he said.

She breathed a silent sigh of relief. The last thing she wanted to do was go running. Running was for four-legged animals who didn't know any better!

She watched him remove his disk from the computer, place it in its envelope, and start for the door. A few seconds later, she was alone.

Alone with an idea.

A way to get back at him, to teach him that *no one* treats Roxanne Easton like that and gets away with it.

A smile spread across her face as she reached for his disk. She removed hers from the computer and, her smile growing even wider, placed his disk in her machine.

Her hands were shaking from anticipation, from the excitement of doing something really terrible to him. She picked up the computer manual and flipped through it. She stopped at the section entitled "How to Copy A Disk."

"This isn't so complicated," she told herself. "What's the big deal?"

Less than five minutes later, she had copied Dick's computer project onto a fresh disk. And after more reading in the manual and a few false tries, she managed to insert her name at the top of the project.

Then she took her project, the simple program Frankie had done for her, and inserted Dick's name at the top.

"Rox, you're only here for two weeks, and already you're a computer genius!" she said aloud.

"What was that?"

Bill Willard appeared in the doorway. "Hey — you still here?"

"I just finished," she said, giving him a warm smile. "I'm really pleased with my project. I hope you are, too."

"I'm sure I will be," he said, returning her smile.

She handed him the two disks. "Here's Dick's project, too," she said. "He had to run out. I really think he should've put a little more time into his. But he just didn't seem to care about the competition."

Willard took the disks from her. "That's too bad," he said. "Hey — you want to go downstairs to the game room and get a cold soda?"

"Great," she said, taking his arm. "I could use something cold after all my hard work."

Chapter 19

"Pamela? Are you up? Telephone."

Her father's voice and the rap on her door broke Pamela's concentration. She sighed, wiped the palette knife on a rag, and balanced it on the ledge of the easel. She was working on a still life with flowers and had been putting in the petals with the edge of the knife.

He knocked again. "Pamela?"

"Coming," she replied. As she reached for the knob, she recalled that she was wearing only an old paint-covered shirt. She grabbed her robe from the back of the door and shrugged it on as she went out.

The upstairs phone was at the head of the stairs in a niche that the builders of the house had probably intended for a statue.

"Hello?"

"I hope I didn't interrupt?" Fiona said hesitantly. "Were you painting?"

"Yes, but it's all right."

"Are you sure? I know how much *I* resent interruptions when I'm working."

"It's okay," Pamela insisted. "I was ready for a break."

"Oh, good. I'm ringing you up to ask if I might come by for a few minutes this morning. I've got a scheme that I hope you'll fall in with."

Pamela smiled. The way Fiona used words was so *British*. "Sure," she replied. "Come over anytime."

Half an hour later Fiona tapped on her door. "Is this your studio?" she said, looking around curiously at the canvases piled against the walls, the paint tubes scattered over the top of the desk, and the vase of dying flowers on the window ledge.

"It's supposed to be my bedroom," Pamela replied with a laugh. "I know it's an awful mess, but when I'm painting I don't notice, and when I'm sleeping I *can't* notice. So it really doesn't matter, does it?"

Fiona laughed. "I suppose not."

"Still, there really isn't anyplace to sit. Why don't we go out in the yard. Now that I think of it, it's kind of hot up here."

As they passed through the kitchen, Pamela poured two glasses of cold grape juice and handed one to Fiona. The grass under the big oak looked cool and lush. Pamela sat down and crossed her legs, then marveled at her companion. Fiona had placed herself on the ground with her legs pointed out to each side so extremely that they almost made a straight line from one set of toes to the other. She looked as if she ought to topple over backward. She seemed remarkably unaware that she was doing anything unusual.

She bent forward at the hips, plucked a blade of grass, and chewed on it for a moment before saying, "I have a favor to ask you. Have I told you anything about our plans for a Midsummer Revel?"

Pamela nodded. "A little. Not much, though."

"Until the last few days there *wasn't* much to tell. But you know how good Jonathan is at inspiring people. We are getting endorsements and support from all over."

"Really? That's great."

Fiona shook her head. "No, it's awful! Everything seems to be getting out of hand! Everyone expects an impressive, polished performance, but we can't possibly give it to them. We're not professionals, after all."

"Of course not," Pamela said warmly, "and it isn't fair of them to expect you to be."

"No, I agree. But I do think we have to do something more ambitious than we had planned at first. Something grander. And we do have more resources now. The reason I came over was to ask you for some help."

"Sure, what do you need? I could paint some posters if you like."

"It's a bit late for that, but what we do need rather desperately are banners for the procession. There's nothing like a banner waving in the wind to give a feeling of occasion."

Pamela's imagination presented her with a picture she couldn't resist: a parade of people winding its way up the hill in Rosemont Park. Over them, silhouetted now against the woods and now against the sky, floated a series of big banners in strong designs and vibrant colors. *Her* designs and colors, *her* banners. When would she have a chance like this again?

"I'd love to do it," she said. "What did you have in mind?"

For the next half hour they swapped ideas and images. Finally Pamela had a fairly clear idea of the task she had taken on. She wasn't going to find it easy, but she was pretty sure that she was going to have a lot of fun.

"Okay," she said, getting to her feet. "I'll take a trip to the mall this afternoon. The Fabric Mart ought to have most of what I need to get started."

Fiona stayed where she was. When Pamela looked down at her in surprise, she plucked another blade of grass and began to tear it into two strips.

"Fiona, there's something else on your mind, isn't there?" Pamela said.

Frowning with effort, Fiona said, "Yes, there is, actually. You may think this is awfully forward of me, Pamela, but I'm concerned about you and

Matt. I like you both so much; I hate to see such a distance developing between you."

"I don't like it, either." Pamela felt herself torn between wanting to share her feelings and resenting her interference. "But it's not all my fault."

"Of course not. And I don't suppose Matt thinks it is his fault, either. Does it really matter who's at fault?"

"Maybe not. It's just that . . . look, do you ever get tired of being with Jonathan, or find yourself wishing he were somebody else?"

"Not more than three or four times a week," Fiona said dryly. "But then, he says something no one else would say, or gives me a certain sort of look, and it's all right again. Is that the way you've been feeling with Matt?"

Pamela sat down on the grass again. "Sometimes I wonder if maybe we've used each other up in some way. I don't even know what I mean. It's just that I used to feel such a sense of excitement whenever I saw him, and it just isn't like that between us anymore."

She broke off in confusion. She had come very close to telling Fiona how she felt when Ben put his arms around her. But she wasn't ready to share that with anyone. She wasn't even sure that she was ready to think too much about it herself.

Fiona didn't seem to notice. "That sort of thing does happen with couples, you know. It hasn't exactly been all roses between me and Jonathan, either. I think if you're patient and ride this thing through, before long everything will be back to normal."

Fiona brought her legs together in front of her, bent her knees, and rose onto her feet in one fluid motion. "Well, I hope you don't think I'm awfully nosy. But after I felt such tension between you two the other day, I thought I ought to say something. It would be a great shame if either of you let anything get in the way of your feelings for each other."

Pamela walked Fiona around to the front, where she had left her bicycle, and watched her pedal off. She certainly hoped Fiona was right. The problem was, she wasn't even sure she still had any feelings left for Matt.

Chapter 20

Matt called on Sunday night, at a few minutes after ten. The moment she heard his voice, Pamela felt a rush of affection for him that surprised her by its intensity. She must have been missing him more than she was letting herself know.

"How are you doing?" he asked.

"Okay, how about you?"

"Okay. I just got off work. I would have called earlier, but we got jammed up with road service calls. Sundays are bad that way."

"Oh." She hesitated, on the edge of asking him once again how he was. What she really wanted to know was, Did he miss her? Did he think about her?

After a moment of silence Pamela said, "I saw Fiona today. She wants me to make banners for the Midsummer Revel. I told her I would."

"I know. She stopped by the station this afternoon."

Pamela filed that fact away for later examination.

"She sounded excited about the Revel," she said.

"Uh-huh. So does Jonathan. I can't really get into it, but maybe I will when I have a little more time to myself." He cleared his throat, and the pitch of his voice rose slightly. "Hey, that reminds me. My uncle gave me the evening off tomorrow. I'll be done at six. Why don't we grab something to eat and go to a movie?"

"Oh, Matt, I wish I could."

"You *can't*?" he asked incredulously.

"No. Tomorrow's our first campfire at Woodlands, and I have to be there. I won't get back to town before eight-thirty, and I told some of the other counselors I'd go to the sub shop with them afterward. I guess I can back out," she added.

"No, that's okay. Some other time."

"Wait a minute. I have an idea. Why don't you meet me at the sub shop at eight-thirty? You can get a bite to eat and meet the gang, and then you and I can go to the movies."

"I don't think — "

"Come on, Matt. Please." She spoke very quickly, to keep him from turning her down. "You know some of the people already, and I know you'll like the others — they're a great bunch — and since we have to eat anyway, why not the sub shop? We can decide on a movie when I see you."

"I don't — " he began again, then said, "okay, if that's what you want."

"What *I* want is to see you," she said, "and it's the best way I can think of. Matt?" She glanced around to make sure her dad and brother weren't nearby, then added in a softer voice, "I love you."

"Yeah, me, too," he replied. "Sleep tight. I'll see you tomorrow night."

She slowly replaced the receiver and walked upstairs to her room. She had wanted to see Matt soon to see if her reaction to him was as she had told Fiona that afternoon. She shuddered at the realization that she'd rather spend the evening with her new friends from camp, and Ben, than with Matt.

In the center of the clearing was a patch of bare earth five feet across surrounded by a circle of stones. At one side, under the trees, a cord of split logs and a big pile of brush waited. Ben stood at the head of the path, watched by a half dozen eager eleven-year-olds, and tried to think what to do.

His group had been chosen by lot to build the campfire today. This was an important and much-envied honor. The only difficulty was that Ben had never built a fire in his life. Even the stove in his kitchen was electric. And the campfire *had* to be a success. If it fizzled, his kids were going to be laughed at for days, and he would lose their respect.

There were two kinds of knowledge, the kind that was passed along from one generation to another, and the kind that you discovered for yourself. No one in his parents' generation had bothered to pass on fire-making skills to him, so it was up to him to reinvent them on the spot. He walked slowly into the clearing, thinking as hard and fast as he ever had during an exam.

What made fires burn? That was easy: oxygen and fuel. So the first point was to be sure the fire got enough oxygen. In other words, air. Air rose as it was heated — that was why hot-air balloons worked. So if he put the air holes near the bottom, the rising air would pull more air in after it, giving the fire a constant supply.

"Hey, Ben, can I start the fire?"

"No, it's my turn!"

"Is not!"

"Is, too!"

"Is not!"

"Hold it!" Ben shouted. "We're all going to build this fire together. Now, there's a science to it, and we're going to learn all about it while we're building this one." He grinned suddenly. "And tonight we'll find out if we did it right. Okay — the first thing a fire needs is air. . . ."

". . . And the twig on the branch,
And the branch on the tree,

And the tree in the ground,
And the green grass grows all around, all around,
The green grass grows all around!"

Pamela had to smile. On each verse, the closer they got to the end, the louder her kids sang, and the more they bounced up and down in rhythm.

Maria turned and gave her a big smile. Her eyes were glistening with joy. Pamela reached over and tousled her sandy blonde hair. These campfires were a great idea. She felt that she had grown closer to the kids in her group in the last forty-five minutes than in the entire week. Look at the way they were clustering around her. Julie, the youngest in her group, would have climbed onto her lap if she had let her.

Frank, the director, was standing in the fire-light where everyone could see him, leading the song. He made funny faces and waved his hands wildly and used his whole body to encourage all the kids to join in.

And on that feather (and on that feather)
There was a flea (there was a flea). . . .

Ben's group was to the left, next to hers. She glanced over. Eliot and Dave, the two cutups who gave her the most hassles in her art classes, looked like little angels in the firelight. Ben met her eyes, nodded toward the center of the clear-ing, and mouthed the words *some fire.* She nodded back and gave him an okay sign.

It *was* some fire. Earlier, when the kids filed into the clearing, they had seen a square structure, about three feet high, that looked like a log cabin filled with brush. Once everyone was seated on the ground, Frank had given a little talk about the importance of fire to man, then thrust a flaming torch into the bottom of the structure.

Pamela had held her breath. Ben had told her how worried he was that he would flunk the test of making the campfire, and she knew from experience how easy it was to have a fire die on you. For five or ten seconds after Frank applied the torch, nothing happened. She was dreadfully aware that the fire was going to be a total flop.

But suddenly there was a soft *chuff*! and the structure burst into orange and yellow flame. Everybody had cheered, and Ben's kids had cheered the loudest.

Now Frank was trying to teach the group a beautiful old Shaker song called " 'Tis the Gift to be Simple." Pamela didn't know the song, but instead of trying to learn the words, she found her thoughts drifting to Matt. She seldom thought of him these days. When she was out here, in the woods, the campers and the other counselors were much more real, more *important*.

She looked down. Maria had moved over and was leaning against her, half asleep. She put her arm around the little girl's shoulders and felt a strange new warmth spread through her. When she blinked, to give her eyes relief from staring at the fire, she discovered that her cheeks were damp. She dried them with the tail of her shirt, then looked up to find Ben watching her. She knew he was remembering, as she was, that other campfire at Laurie's party, and the first kisses they exchanged. She wished that everyone would disappear, just for a moment, so that she and Ben could be in each other's arms again.

During the school year, the sub shop was the favorite hangout for practically everybody at Kennedy High. During the summer it changed. The Cardinals' football pennants still fluttered from the rafters, the motorcycle still hung on the wall, the stuffed bear, and the tall carved statue of an Indian still guarded the approach to the jukebox, but the noise level was lower and the mood less frenetic. It was even possible to carry on a conversation without having to shout or read lips.

The group of counselors from Camp Woodlands had taken over one of the long picnic tables in the center of the room. They were dividing their attention between an exchange of information about some of the campers and the sandwiches and fries in front of them.

Pamela was listening to the conversation with only half an ear. Each time the door opened she looked over, expecting to see Matt walk in.

Ben made a strangled noise that drew Pamela's attention. She looked from him back to the door and saw a group of four or five people standing just inside the shop, choosing a table. One of them was Elise Hammond. Ben muttered something, stood up, and went over to her. Their conversation didn't last more than a minute or two. When he returned to his seat, he looked both puzzled and angry.

"Are you okay?" Pamela whispered.

"Me? Sure." He straightened up and tried to smile.

Before she could say anything else, Matt stepped in the door. Her heart sank. He was still in his work clothes — jeans with grease-stained knees, a blue short-sleeved shirt, also grease-stained, with *Matt* embroidered in red script above the right-hand pocket, and thick-soled, steel-toed boots. His hands were grimy, and he sported a black smear on his left cheek.

But none of that bothered her nearly as much as the invisible but obvious chip on his shoulder. The way he was standing, feet apart, hands shoved into his pants pockets, like the expression on his face, said that he expected people to put him down, and he dared them to try it. She had often seen him like this when she was first getting to know him, but she had thought that was all in the past. Hadn't he learned anything? Didn't he realize that when he showed people who he really was, they didn't despise him, they respected and liked him?

He looked over at her. She waved and pointed to the seat next to her. He nodded expressionlessly, walked across the room, and stood at the foot of the table.

"Hi," she said brightly. "I waited to order till you got here. I'm getting a special sub. Do you want to split an order of fries?"

"No, thanks," he said. "I'm not hungry."

"Oh. Well . . . do you want something to drink while I'm eating? I didn't have dinner yet."

He shook his head. "I'm not thirsty, either."

By now the others at the table were watching and listening, though the more polite of them tried to pretend that they weren't by looking in another direction. From the other side of the room, Ben's friend Elise was staring, too.

"Well, have a seat, then," Pamela said desperately, "and let me introduce the gang. Everybody, this is Matt Jacobs. Let's see, you know Ben; Erin, and that's Andy over there, and Chuck, and this is Nancy."

Matt nodded silently and stayed on his feet. When the chorus of hi's died down, he said to Pamela, "You go ahead and eat. I don't have time to hang around tonight."

She stared at him in astonishment. Didn't they have a date to go to a movie? What was going on? He refused to meet her eyes, and instead stared steadily at his feet.

"See you around," he added to the rest of the table, and turned to go.

Pamela excused herself, scrambled out of her seat, and followed Matt through the door. As soon as they were outside, she grabbed his arm and said, "Matt Jacobs, what did you think you were doing in there, humiliating me in front of my friends? What's wrong with you?"

He shook his arm loose and glared at her. "If you're ashamed to be seen with me, there's an easy way to fix that. I just don't feel like hanging around with a bunch of strangers right now."

Afterward, she thought of how she might have answered him. She could have said that they weren't really her friends but the people she worked with. She could have reassured him that she wasn't ashamed of him. She might have asked why he was so upset, or why he was canceling their date without any notice. She might have done a lot of things if she had kept her temper and presence of mind. But the way he was treating her threw her into a cold rage.

Her nostrils flared and her eyes narrowed. Pressing her lips together hard, she stared at him for a long moment. Then she whirled around and ran back into the sub shop.

Chapter 21

Elise tied off the long, thin braid with an elastic band and looped it around the back of her friend's head, where the other three braids were pinned. She did some delicate adjustments to get the four loops, two at the side, to hang to the right height, then said. "Okay, take a look."

Emily Stevens stood up and went to the mirror. Elise had parted her long dark hair in the center before braiding the front locks and carrying them around the sides. The style made her oval face look very old-fashioned and severe.

"I like it," she told Elise, "but I think it's a little too formal. I'd have to wear a floor-length gown with this hairdo."

"Hmm. What if we worked narrow ribbons into the braids?"

"Well . . . maybe. Let's try it next time. It'll

take too long to do these braids again. Come on, it's my turn. Where's the mousse?"

Over the next half hour, Elise had a chance to see how she looked with her hair upswept, downswept, sideswept, and windswept. Emily went full-out on her, trying everything from a fifties look to an asymmetrical topknot that made her feel like a creature from another planet. Finally she brushed it out, patted it in a couple of places, and said, "There."

Elise looked in the mirror once again. This time her familiar self looked back at her. It was both a comfort and a disappointment. Somewhere in a childish part of her mind she had hoped that changing her look would change *her*. But it hadn't. All her longings, all her feelings of doubt and confusion were still with her. Without intending to, she gave a long, heartfelt sigh.

"Hey, it's not *that* bad, is it?" Emily said.

Elise shook her head. "I don't know. It just might be."

"Hey, it's pretty warm in here. Let's go out in the backyard and cool off."

The night was clear and the moon was not yet up. To the east, the lights of Washington turned the sky a yellowish gray, but overhead it was the darkest of blues and sprinkled with stars. The two friends sat on the grass and listened to a silence broken only by tree frogs and a distant airplane.

"I haven't seen Ben lately," Emily said in an

offhand voice. "How is his camp job working out?"

"Oh, he loves it," Elise said.

She did her best to keep the sarcasm out of her voice, but Emily's sensitivity to such things had won her the reputation of being Kennedy High's Dear Abby.

"Are you two having problems?" she asked quietly.

"*I'm* having problems. If you want to know about him, you'll have to ask him yourself. He's so caught up in that camp and those people he's working with that I haven't seen him lately, either. Not that I care that much," she admitted.

"Well, it's always hard to find enough time when you have a lot of interests, isn't it? From what you said, you're pretty busy yourself."

"That's true," Elise said, "but I think I'd make time for Ben if he wanted me to. I wouldn't be off at some museum or having an important meeting with one of the counselors who just happens to be a certain girl in our class. Meetings, he calls them. At least I don't try to kid myself."

Emily cleared her throat. After a moment, she said, "What if he does want you to make time for him but is scared to say so?"

"Ben? Give me a break! He'd tell me. He's not as shy as he used to be. He's good at going after what he wants. That's what worries me — what he wants. Because I don't think it's me anymore."

She found herself on the verge of tears. She

swallowed, sniffed, and dabbed at the corners of her eyes.

Emily reached over and gave her hand a squeeze, and then Elise *did* start crying.

"It was such a terrible mistake," Elise said when she thought she could speak again. "Ben's been my best friend for as long as I can remember. I could always count on him. Why did I ever let us start going out?"

"Well? Why did you?"

"I couldn't help it. I woke up one day and discovered that I'd fallen in love with him. He said the same thing happened to him, too. Maybe it did, but it's different now. All I know is that it's not working out for us as a couple, and I'm terrified that I'll end up losing him as a friend, too."

Emily was silent for a long time. When Elise glanced over at her, she was looking up at the sky. Her forehead was wrinkled, and she seemed to be thinking very hard. At last she said, "There's something you're leaving out, isn't there? What about the way you feel about Ben? Has that changed, too?"

Elise was startled by her friend's perceptiveness. Maybe Emily could help her understand the feelings she'd been finding so confusing lately.

"Maybe," she said in a voice just above a whisper. "I don't turn to jelly when I see him, the way I used to. I don't lie awake, unable to sleep because his face and voice haunt my thoughts. Last night I had a meeting with some of the hospital volunteers at the sub shop, and when

I walked in, he was there with some people from camp. I held my meeting anyway and remembered what I had to do and talked over the program just as if he weren't sitting ten feet away. Maybe I know him *too* well. I mean, how romantic can you feel about a boy you shared a blanket with in nursery school?"

Emily laughed, but then turned serious. "Sometimes old friends *aren't* as exciting as new ones," she said. "There's a special thrill in getting to know somebody and letting him get to know you. I guess it's like going to live in a foreign country — everything's new and strange and exciting."

"Oh, I know! And I never had that with Ben because I already knew him so well. That's why — " She broke off suddenly. She had come very close to telling Emily about Matt Jacobs. She hadn't been able to go on with her meeting at the sub shop when *he* walked in, that was for sure. She hadn't been able to stop looking at him for a moment. And when he got into that fight with Pamela, she had had to hold on to her chair to keep from moving closer to listen in. At the same time she had wanted to hide her face because she was sure that she was somehow to blame for the fight.

Emily had obviously noticed her broken-off thought and followed where it had been going. "It must be very confusing," she said, looking off across the neighbor's yard. "Ben means such a lot to you but he can't be everything, can he? And to find somebody else who gives you something that he doesn't. . . . Well, what do you do?"

"I wish I knew," Elise sighed. "If only I could feel those sparks again when Ben kisses me, the way I used to! Not all of them, maybe, but at least a few! That isn't asking too much, is it? But instead I find myself thinking about things I have to do at the office the next day, or what I had for supper, or almost anything except the guy who's kissing me. It doesn't have to be that way, Em. I *know* it doesn't! When Matt — "

There was a long silence. Finally Emily said in a neutral voice, "Matt from school? Doesn't his girl friend work at the same camp as Ben?"

"That has nothing to do with it! I didn't even remember that when I met him!"

"Does Ben know?"

She shook her head stubbornly. "There isn't anything to know. And anyway, he and Pamela. . . . Look, Matt and I talk on the phone a lot, and now and then he gives me a lift when Mom is using her car."

"Well, what's it like? How do you feel about him?"

Elise gave a short laugh. "When I see him I practically melt. I can't help it," she added more vigorously. "When he touches my hand, I start tingling all over, and when I imagine him kissing me. . . . "

"And you don't think there's anything to know? Come on, Elise, this sounds serious!"

"Well, I don't really think it is yet, but I'm

scared it might get that way. And then I think about Ben, and I get twice as scared. Why does it have to be so difficult?"

Emily reached over to take her friend's hand again. "I don't know," she said in a sympathetic voice. "Maybe it's like a kid who's hooked on candy. You can tell him all about cavities, and not getting the vitamins he needs, and all that, but it doesn't matter. He knows how sweet candy is. Well, falling in love is like that. It's one of the greatest things around. But there's something even better, and that's *being* in love."

"But I still love Ben, Em. I think I always have and always will. But what happened to the romance in our relationship? It's not my fault it's gone. I know it isn't, because I can still feel a thrill the way I used to — only not with him."

"Look," Emily said, "I don't really know Matt, and I don't know what's going to happen. Maybe you and he will have something really good together. But you can't judge by how it feels when you're first getting to know each other. It all feels new and exciting, but sometimes the only thing that's exciting about it is that it *is* new. Once that wears off, there's nothing left."

"I know," Elise said, "I know. But sometimes it feels like that's what happened with Ben. Half the time I want to finish his sentences for him because I already know what he's going to say."

"But you also know that what he says is going to be funny and bright. You two go back a long, long way; longer than just about anybody I know.

You wouldn't have stayed friends if there wasn't a lot holding you together. Don't forget that."

"I won't," Elise said. "But I wonder if I'll end up with anything besides that memory."

"I want to remember tonight forever!" Laurie exclaimed. She got out of the car, then as an afterthought, slipped off her shoes, and tossed them into the backseat. "Come on, Rick, let's go wading!"

The moon, just above the horizon, cast a glittering path across the water. Without waiting to see if Rick was behind her, Laurie ran down the beach toward the surf as if she had taken an oath to follow that quicksilver moonpath to its source. Once she was ankle-deep, however, she let out a startled squeal and retreated to above the tide line. In the heat of the afternoon the water had felt refreshingly cool, but by night it was cold enough to make her numb.

She gave a little shiver. The club they had just come from was supposed to have been air-conditioned, but it hadn't made much difference. A couple of hundred kids were jammed in there, all dancing as if a pack of demons was waiting to carry off anyone who stopped or even slowed down. After the first hour, it was hot enough to make the candles on the tables droop. The only way to beat the heat was to ignore it and dance harder, or as Peter Lacey was so fond of saying, "Bop till you drop!"

She had done her best, and that was pretty

darn good. It helped to know that everybody in the place was watching them. Not that Rick was much of a dancer, but with a body like his he didn't need to be. All he had to do was stand in the middle of the floor and do a little flex and ripple, and all the girls were eyeing him with awe. She had had to work a little harder to earn her due, but a hot new outfit from Rezato in Georgetown and a really terrific hairstyle that Ursula had dreamed up for her had made her stand out even before the music started.

The night breeze touched her damp blouse and made her shiver again. Where was Rick? She wanted to warm up in his arms. She looked around but he was nowhere in sight. The car was still there, though. That was reassuring. How far could he have strayed on foot? Then she remembered who he was and what he was training for, and realized that the answer was, very far indeed.

What was that speck way down the beach? As she strained to make it out, it drew closer and grew larger, and she saw that it was Rick. A couple of minutes later he came to a stop next to her. "It's fun running by moonlight," he said. "The shadows make it kind of hard, though. I nearly broke an ankle about half a mile back."

"I like it in the moonlight, too," Laurie said in a sultry voice. She put her hand on his shoulder and looked up into his eyes. The moment he put his arms around her, she meant to fall back as if overcome by emotion. Not that it would be such a pretense. Just being this close to him was giving her the strangest feelings — alternating waves of heat and cold sweeping through her.

He looked at her with passionate interest. "You know, Laurie," he said, "you've given me something important. This means a lot to me."

She was about to say "Me, too" when he continued.

"I never even thought of training by moonlight. It's like I just discovered another four or five hours that I'd never paid any attention to before. And nothing's more valuable than time, right?"

"Right," she said faintly, taking a step closer to him. She would have moved even closer, but there wasn't enough room.

"Laurie?" His voice smoldered with emotion.

"Yes, Rick?" She leaned against him.

"I want to press you."

She figured out that was his way of saying he wanted to take her in his arms. As she was about to reach up and put her arms around his neck, he bent down and grabbed her under the knees with one hand while his other clasped her upper arm. Suddenly, without any warning, he turned her sideways and lifted her up, first to the level of his chest, then over his head. She let out a dismayed screech. She wanted to flail about with her arms and legs, but what if she accidentally made him drop her?

He looked up at her. "Say, Laurie, how much do you weigh?"

"None of your business! Let me down!"

He frowned in concentration. "About a hundred pounds or so? People are a lot harder to press than free weights. The handles aren't as easy to grab. Still, it's kind of different, isn't it? Maybe it could become a regular event, to get publicity. What do you think?"

"I think you're going to be very sorry if you don't let me down *right now*!"

"Huh? Oh, sure."

She felt as if she had stepped into a runaway elevator. The ride ended an instant later on the sand. She got to her feet ready to go at him tooth and nail, but he looked so pleased with himself, and with her, that her anger seemed pointless. And it *had* been a remarkable experience, though not exactly the one she had been expecting.

"Come on, Rick," she said, slipping her hand around his waist. "Let's go for a walk on the beach. Maybe we can sit on the sand and watch the moon rise."

"It's up already," he said in a puzzled voice.

"I know, *I know*!" She took his hand and put it around her shoulders. "Come on!"

"Well, okay. If you're sure you wouldn't rather run."

Laurie closed her eyes, ground her teeth, and wondered if this was worth it. But then she remembered the way he looked running along the beach. "I'm sure," she said.

Chapter 22

Pamela looked at the knot of kids and gulped. Sixteen campers and three counselors were scheduled to go on the day hike to Indian Falls, and Frank had put her in charge. The kids milled around, talking and giggling. On the outskirts, one boy snatched another's Orioles baseball cap and ran off laughing with the other close behind him. Pamela caught the eye first of Erin, then of Ben, and mouthed the word "Ready?" They both nodded.

She climbed up onto a tree stump and blew a short blast on her whistle. The crowd quieted down and looked at her. "Okay, gang," she said loudly. "We're going to have a terrific time today, but we all have to cooperate with each other to make it work." She looked slowly around the circle of faces. "Please, no wandering off on your own. Stay with the group all the time. Okay?"

About half the campers murmured yes. The rest nodded.

"Great."

Eliot raised his hand. "What if we meet a bear?"

Most of the kids laughed, but Pamela thought she heard an edge of nervousness in the laughter. She glanced at Ben.

"We won't," he said with a smile. "The last bear in these woods got transferred to West Virginia before you were born."

"But there *could* be a bear," Dave insisted. "Or some other kind of wild animal."

"Bears, no. Deer, porcupines, raccoons, skunks, maybe even a bobcat, but no bears. Too bad, I like bears. And we probably won't even see any of the others, though we might hear one or two running away through the underbrush. They're a lot more scared of us than we are of them."

"Thanks, Ben," Pamela said. "Erin?"

Erin was one of the swimming counselors and also taught a minicourse in first aid for the campers. "Indian Falls is a beautiful place," she began, "but it's off in the middle of the forest. We're all going to have to follow a few simple rules, and the most important one is, *no horseplay*. If you want to wade in the pool at the bottom of the falls, fine. I'll probobly be right there beside you. But no teasing or shoving, no swimming, and *no* climbing on the rocks. We want this to be a fun trip, and that means a safe trip. Any questions?"

The kids shook their heads and looked impressed by her seriousness. Then Caitlin raised her hand and said, "How long is it to lunch?" That really drew a laugh. Caitlin was a skinny eleven-year-old who had one of the biggest appetites in the whole camp.

Pamela joined the laughter, then said, "The sooner we leave, the sooner we get to the Falls and have lunch. Everybody ready? Line up single file behind Erin. I'll be in the middle and Ben will bring up the rear. An-n-d we're *off*!"

She jumped down from the stump as the kids sent up a cheer.

Their high spirits made the hikers a noisy bunch, but gradually the forest worked its magic on them. They talked to each other in low voices and moved with a deliberation quite different from their usual tearing around. The loudest sound was the rustle of the leaves as nineteen pairs of sneakers crossed the leaf-strewn path, and the occasional limb brushing against an arm or leg. When some small unseen creature scurried off through the bushes as they passed, they jumped at the sudden noise, then laughed at themselves for jumping.

Pamela glanced down at her watch. They should be getting close to the clearing Frank had told her about. A good place for a snack break and a short rest, he had said. The path had already led them past a couple of open places, but she was looking for one with a big lightning-blasted oak in the center, on a low hillock, and a Forest Service equipment shed near the edge, almost hidden by the trees.

Up at the front of the line, Erin came to a halt at a fork in the path and looked back at Pamela. Pulling the trail map from her shirt pocket, Pamela walked forward and looked over the situation. The branch to the right looked more heavily traveled, but there was nothing else to indicate which was the main trail. She studied the map for a few moments. She knew pretty well where they must be, and nowhere in the area did their path go left at a fork. The trail to the right had to be the correct one.

"Anything I can do?" Ben asked.

She looked up in surprise. She had assumed that he was still at the back of the line. Then she saw that there wasn't any back to the line. All the kids were crowding near her, waiting to hear which way to go.

"No, I don't think so," she said. "Okay, Erin," she added, raising her voice slightly, "we go to the right. And everybody watch for splashes of yellow paint on the trees. We ought to see one in the next hundred feet or so."

One of the younger boys moved closer to her and said, "Pamela, are we lost?"

The others became very quiet.

"Of course not, Sean," she replied with a smile. She was nervous, but she couldn't let the campers see that.

"But you were looking at the map. That's what most people do when they're lost."

"We're right on track, Sean. And besides you've got it completely backward, silly! People look at maps to *keep* from getting lost."

"Not my daddy. He *never* looks at a map unless he's lost."

"That's why he gets lost all the time," one of the kids shouted. The others guffawed, and Sean turned pink.

"Never mind," Pamela said, patting him on the shoulder. "We're not even a little bit lost, and we're almost to the place where we're going to have a rest and a snack, so the sooner we get moving, the better."

As the kids fell into line again behind Erin, she found herself wishing that she dared cross her fingers. She knew perfectly well that they weren't lost, but even the faintest possible doubt was made overwhelming by the fact that Frank had placed her in charge of these kids. Why, she didn't know, but he had. She was responsible for them.

Up ahead, Erin waved her arm, pointed to the yellow paint on a tree alongside the path, and grinned. Pamela grinned back. As a matter of habit, she counted the kids in front of her, then turned to count those behind her. Eight in front, seven behind. She frowned. She must have miscounted. This time she stepped to the side of the path, where she could see them all more clearly. There were eight kids on the path between Erin and her, and between her and Ben there were —

Her mouth fell open, and her breath seemed to catch in her throat. She quickly counted again, but she already knew what she would find.

"HALT!"

Everyone — Erin and Ben included — stared at her as if she had just lost her mind. Then Ben hurried over to her. "What is it?" he demanded. "What's wrong?"

Fear had made her mouth too dry to speak. She swallowed once, then again, and whispered, "Somebody's missing. We've lost a child."

Ben's eyes widened. "No way!" he said. He looked around quickly.

"Keep your voice down; don't alarm them." She straightened up and said in a louder voice, "Okay, guys, let's all line up. Time for a surprise head count." To Ben and Erin she said, "Each of you start at your end and work your way to the other end, okay? I'm staying right here."

As the other two counselors quickly counted the line, she tried to suppress her growing feeling of panic and make a plan. She knew what Ben and Erin would find even before she saw their grim faces.

"Fifteen," Erin said. Ben nodded.

"Okay, who is it?" She scanned the faces of the children, who were starting to catch the mood of fear from their counselors. One face, though, did not look frightened at all. In fact, there was even a badly hidden hint of smug anticipation in the expression. "Eliot," she called. "Would you please come here?"

"Dave's missing," Ben muttered to her.

"I know," she muttered back.

"I'll murder that little imp!"

"First we find him," she replied, "then we murder him."

Eliot had stopped just in front of them and was watching them warily. He was very experienced at getting into trouble and just as skilled at keeping cool and avoiding the consequences. Usually, though, he had his buddy with him for support. Being on his own like this seemed to unnerve him.

"I didn't do anything!" he exclaimed before any of the counselors could speak.

"No one said you did," Pamela said. "We need your help, Eliot. Where is Dave?"

His eyes shifted. "I don't know," he said sullenly.

"He's not in the line with the rest of us, is he? He must have left the path, then, or stayed behind. Do you know where he went, Eliot? Or how long ago?"

"Or why?" Ben interjected.

"I don't know," the boy repeated.

Pamela knelt down until her eyes were on the same level as his. He tried to stare at his feet, but she placed her hand under his chin and gently forced him to meet her gaze.

"Eliot," she said softly, "this is very important. Dave is your friend. He's out there in the woods somewhere. By now he's lost and very scared. He may even be hurt. He's our friend, too, and we want to find him. But we need your help. We can't start looking for him unless we know which way he went."

All the smugness was gone from Eliot's face, replaced by a growing alarm, but he still kept his lips pressed tightly closed.

Erin had a try. "Look, the longer we wait to start looking, the more lost he'll be, and the harder it will be to find him."

"That's right," Ben added. "And what a terrific thing to be able to help find somebody who's gotten lost."

Eliot's eyes darted from one of them to the other. Almost frantically he said, "It wasn't my idea! I told him I thought it was dumb!"

"What was Dave planning to do?" Pamela asked as calmly as she could.

"It was back there when we stopped by the other path. He decided to sneak up ahead and hide by the path. Then when we came along he was going to make noises like a bear and scare everybody. Probably he's up there right now waiting for us. He's not going to like me squealing on him like this."

"If he *is* up there," Ben said. "It's pretty easy to get lost in the woods unless you're following a path."

Eliot turned pale, as if he were just beginning to understand the kind of trouble his friend was in. As his lower lip started to tremble, Pamela reached out and squeezed his arm. "Don't worry, Eliot," she said. "We'll find him. I promise you."

As she got to her feet, she met Ben's eyes. He

was obviously wondering exactly how she was going to fulfill her promise. So was she.

The branch flipped from her hand and lashed her across the cheek, then tangled itself in her hair. Still bent over almost double, she patiently freed herself and continued through the narrow gap between the bushes. At last she was able to straighten up. Her back ached, but there wasn't time to think about that. *Where was Dave?*

"Dave," she shouted through cupped hands, "where are you?" Her eyes searched in a semicircle in front of her. Off to the left, just visible through the trees, Ben shouted, too, then waved to her. He was still even with her, then. Reassured, she continued to walk in what she hoped was a straight line. The child couldn't have gone very far before they started to search for him. They would certainly find him soon.

How could she have let this happen? Her first time in charge, and one of her kids got lost. She should have brought up the rear herself, so that she could keep an eye on all of them the whole time. At the very least she should have put Dave and Eliot where she could watch them. She knew they were born troublemakers. She should have realized that they were bound to get into mischief and taken precautions. If anything happened to Dave. . . . But that was silly. Nothing was going to happen. They were bound to find him soon.

Ben shouted and waved. Filled with wild hope,

she hurried in his direction, but before she had taken more than a few steps she knew that his news, whatever it was, was not the news she wanted to hear. She pushed through a tangle of branches and found herself at the top of a steep brush-covered bank. At the bottom, a stream glittered in the sunlight.

"Can I see that map again?" Ben said. She handed it to him, then looked over his shoulder. He pointed with his forefinger. "We must be about here. There's the trail, and here's this stream, roughly parallel to it. That's our first piece of good luck."

"It is? Why?"

"Figure Dave got turned around once he was in the woods. If he found the stream, he'd know not to cross it, and if he found the trail, he'd know to stay on it. So he's somewhere between the trail and the stream. The only question is, upstream or downstream? We could separate and try both directions."

"No!" Pamela's response was instinctive and emphatic.

"Okay," he said, just as promptly. It occurred to her that he didn't relish the idea of separating, either. "Then I vote for downstream. That's the direction back to camp. If I got myself lost, I think I'd try to go the way I thought home was. I wouldn't keep pushing on into the unknown."

"Assuming you knew which way was which."

"Right." He glanced around, and for one moment his face looked so young and frightened that she longed to give him a hug of comfort and reassurance.

Instead, she tried to be practical. “You keep near the stream,” she said, “and I’ll go along farther in the woods. Even if we don’t see him, maybe he’ll hear us shouting.”

She was turning away when a tiny patch of white caught her eyes amid all the greens and browns. What could it be? Probably a scrap of paper, or a discarded sandwich wrapper blown there from somebody’s picnic. Was it worth a look?

“I’m going over there for a minute,” she said, glancing at Ben. When she looked back, the patch of white was no longer visible. Frowning, she made her way over to where she thought it had been and was stopped by a tangled wall of thorny branches. She circled it to the left and then to the right without finding anything white.

She was on the point of going back to resume the search when she noticed a low opening in the thicket. It looked as if it had been made by an animal. She bent down and peered in cautiously. The area inside was deeply shaded, patterned confusingly with random speckles of light, but she was sure she saw a form on the ground. A fawn, maybe? or —

“Dave!” she cried. The form moved. “Dave! Are you all right?”

He slowly raised his head to look at her. Across his dirt-stained cheeks, tears had washed tracks of white. His lips moved, but she couldn't hear the words.

"What?" She began to crawl through the low tunnel toward him.

"I was hiding," he said faintly. "I thought you'd be mad."

"Oh, Dave," she said with tears in her eyes. "I'm not mad. I'm just happy you're okay."

"I hurt my knee. I got scared and started running and then I tripped and fell. I tried to walk, but I couldn't. I was afraid a bear would get me."

"It's all right now. Ben and I are here. We'll get you back to camp and get your knee taken care of. Can you move?"

He managed to crawl out of his hiding place, but when he tried to stand up, his face went pale, and he cried out in pain. Pamela blew her whistle three times, then three times again, to signal that they had found him, but she didn't think they could wait until the party from camp located them. Their only real choice was to carry him out of the woods.

Ben had once learned how to form a fireman's seat by interlacing four arms. After some experimenting, they managed to hoist Dave up and start toward the trail, but it was terribly hard work. With no hands free, they had to circle around brushy areas instead of pushing through, so the journey out of the woods was many times longer than the walk in had been. By the time they stumbled onto the trail, Pamela was moving like a robot, one foot then the other, ignoring the tiredness in her legs and the searing pain in her arms.

They set Dave down by the side of the trail, then slumped to the ground themselves. Pamela lay flat, aching arms outstretched, and tried to breathe deeply and slowly. Finally she felt able to sit up and take care of Dave, but when she looked over, she discovered that the boy, worn out by the stress of his experience, had fallen asleep. She nudged Ben and pointed.

"Fine time for a nap," he muttered.

She started to laugh, and in the sudden release of tension her laughter turned to tears. Suddenly, Ben's arm was around her shoulders, but that wasn't enough to stop her from shaking. She turned toward him and wrapped her arms around his back, pressing her forehead against his chest. He was holding her tightly with both arms, and he, too, was shaking with emotion. Shocked, she looked up and saw tears in his eyes.

"I was so scared that he would be hurt," he whispered. "I've never been so scared before."

"Me, either. But it's all over now, Ben. It's all right."

At her gentle urging, he lay back against the grassy bank with her close in his arms. Gradually the shaking stopped and they both began to relax. And then a moment came when she realized that they were beginning to find more than comfort in each other. The arms clasping her were not just any arms, they were *his* arms, and the heart pounding so close beneath her ear was his heart.

He stirred. When she raised her head, he was looking at her with an expression of combined affection and bewilderment. "Pamela?" he said.

"Shhh," she whispered, then slowly lowered her lips onto his. His arms tightened around her, pressing her to him with a sudden intensity. She relaxed. She felt as she had at the beach when a breaking wave grabbed her and tumbled her with irresistible force. First the swelling, roaring power, then the sense of being out of control and about to drown, then an amazing moment of floating peacefully to the surface as the wave passed.

This time she was not alone in it. The wave had done its work on Ben, too. She reached over and stroked his cheek. He caught her hand and kissed the palm, sending ripples of sensation up her arm. Then his lips met hers again in a gentle, searching kiss.

Chapter 23

"I don't believe it! I don't believe it!" Roxanne screamed happily. She jumped up and hugged Frankie.

"I don't believe it, either!" Frankie said, with a lot less enthusiasm. "Congratulations, Rox. I knew you could do it."

At the final camp meeting, it had just been announced that Roxanne Easton had won the computer programming competition. Everyone applauded as Roxanne jumped up and down and hugged her friend joyfully. Then the meeting broke up, and the campers headed to their bunks to pack up and prepare to leave.

"I owe you one, Frankie," Roxanne said. "Ask me anything. I'll do it."

"Okay," Frankie said. "Don't ever mention this again."

Roxanne laughed. "Very funny."

"I'm serious," Frankie insisted. "What we did wasn't right, and you know it, Rox. I did all the work for you while you had a good time chasing after Dick Westergard."

"I didn't chase after him," Rox corrected her. "And I know how hard you worked on this project for me. I won't forget it. Wow. Just think how surprised my mom will be when she sees this certificate. She'll never be able to say that I don't work hard enough to succeed again."

"But, Rox, you didn't work hard. I did," Frankie insisted.

"I know, I know." Roxanne gave her an annoyed look. "What do you want — blood? I said, I'll pay you back some day."

She should only know the truth, Roxanne thought. It wasn't even her project that won. It was really Dick's. So much for Frankie's hard work. She's a good friend, though. And good friends like her are hard to find.

Roxanne smiled at Frankie. "Thanks again. Really," she said softly. "You're great."

Frankie shrugged. She knew Roxanne well enough by now to know that her compliments weren't worth a whole lot. But, in a way, it felt good to know that her hard work had paid off. I actually won that competition over everyone else in this camp, she told herself, even if no one else knows it.

"Hey, Rox — we've got to pack up. My parents will be here in less than half an hour," she said.

"Okay. I'll be right there." Roxanne saw Dick across from the boys' cabins. He was leaning against a tree, staring wistfully into the woods.

Frankie hurried off to their bunk. Roxanne began walking quickly toward Dick. She couldn't decide whether to gloat about her victory or be sympathetic. But when she got nearer and saw how upset and disappointed he looked, she decided to play it sympathetic.

Lost in his own thoughts, he didn't see her at first. "Dick?" she called softly, and touched his shoulder.

"What?" He was startled out of his daze. "Oh. It's you. Hi."

"Hi," she said. She kept her hand on his shoulder.

"I guess I should say congratulations," he said, looking back to the woods. "Well . . . congratulations."

"Thanks. I can see you're really disappointed."

"Disappointed isn't the word for it," he said. "I guess I was just overconfident or something. I really expected to win."

"It's all my fault," she said, her voice trembling.

That made him turn to look at her. "What do you mean? How can it be your fault?"

"I took up too much of your time. I was selfish. I was so attracted to you, I liked you so much, I just lost sight of what we were really here for. I distracted you. I kept you from concentrating. I'm sorry, Dick. Really. I guess I made a horrible nuisance of myself and spoiled everything for you."

"Hey, don't blame yourself," he said. "That's silly. Look. You won. You won the competition. You didn't lose sight of what we were here for. *I* did. I blew it. Me. Myself. I. Not you. I just wasn't good enough, I guess."

"Stop it," she said tenderly, pressing her forehead against his shoulder. "It's just a silly competition. I got lucky, that's all. Maybe Willard picked my project because he thinks I'm cute. It doesn't matter. Camp is over. Now it's time to go back to our real lives."

Dick took her chin in his hand and looked into her green eyes. His somber expression slowly gave way to a smile. "You're very smart," he said.

She laughed. "That's the nicest thing you've said to me in days."

"And I'm very stupid," he added. This girl is wonderful, he thought. I must have been out of my mind when I decided I had to give her up. She's smart, she's so understanding, she's so beautiful. . . .

"I've been acting like an idiot," he said.

"What do you mean?"

"I mean, toward you. I've been terrible."

"That's okay," she said, shyly looking at the ground. "Really. I understood."

"Well, I didn't understand," he said, pulling

her close to him. "I didn't understand my own feelings, I guess. I never meant to hurt you. It was just that I thought that I was — "

"Are you gonna shut up and kiss me?" she asked.

They both laughed. They couldn't stop laughing even while they were kissing.

This was so easy, she thought, congratulating herself. This was so much easier than I thought.

"When I get back home, I'll break up with Laurie right away," he whispered in her ear.

"Yes," she whispered back and kissed his cheek.

"I'll call you as soon as I break up with her," he said, and kissed her again.

She pulled away. "I've gotta run. There's Frankie's parents' car, and I haven't even packed. 'Bye."

Waving to Frankie's parents, she began running to her bunk. " 'Bye, I'll call you right away!" Dick called after her.

He could still feel her warm lips on his cheek.

Chapter 24

At the edge of the parking lot, Brenda was helping Pamela assemble the banners she had made for the Midsummer Revel. All they had to do was wrap the outer edges of each one around a long bamboo pole and then staple it in place, but Pamela looked almost frantic with anxiety. As they finished fastening each banner to its pole, they unfurled it and held it up to look at before putting it to one side.

Fiona was unbelievably impressed. She had seen some of Pamela's paintings and loved them, but the banners by their very size made a much stronger impression on her. Some of them were painted and others were more like collages. All of them, however abstract, celebrated nature and its blossoming at midsummer. Birds exchanged fantastic flowers with each other; raccoons and deer danced in a green field; a child sat on a high limb of a tree and raised her arms to the sky in a gesture of joy and thanks. Fiona's favorite was the most abstract of all — an expanse of dark blue cloth, with a semicircular wedge of blue-green felt glued to the lower left corner and a large circle of bright yellow rimmed with white in the upper right.

"Pamela, they're utterly gorgeous!" she exclaimed.

"Thanks," Pamela said. She looked tired. "I wanted to try a couple of other ideas, too, but there wasn't enough time."

"You've done wonderfully. Would you be willing to carry one of your banners at the head of the procession?" She pointed to her favorite.

Pamela smiled. "You like that one? I was afraid it might be too modern for an event like this. I call it 'Honor the Sun.' "

"It reminds me of a photo taken from space," said Brenda. "May I hold the other pole with you?"

"Yes, I'd like that," Pamela replied.

Fiona looked at her curoiusly. She had taken it for granted that Matt would be Pamela's partner in carrying the banner. He was standing not far away with his hands in his pockets, talking to Jonathan, but he never glanced in their direction, and Pamela didn't look his way. She had thought that they had settled their differences, but now she wasn't even sure that they were speaking to each other.

* * *

Pamela had never known that she could have such different feelings at the same time. Carrying her own banner, her "Honor the Sun," at the front of the long procession up the hill had been a solemn moment. And when she looked back and saw her other banners floating above the laughing, dancing crowd, the joy she felt left her faint. She wanted to shout aloud, to hold her arms out like wings and run in smaller and smaller circles until she fell laughing helplessly to the ground.

Ahead, a knot of kids in colorful jerkins were fencing with cardboard mailing tubes. One of them, flailing wildly, backed into her and fell, nearly knocking her down. His opponent courteously lowered his weapon and offered a hand. Behind the flowers and rainbow painted on his cheeks and forehead she recognized Eliot, so she was not surprised to find that it was Dave who was sitting on her foot.

"Arise, Sir David," she said. "Lord Eliot awaits you."

He glanced up, startled, and scrambled to his feet. "Hi, Pamela," he said, and flashed her a heartbreaking smile before he raised his mailing tube and plunged back into the fray.

"*There* you are," said Fiona, who had Matt in tow. "Come along. We're about to do the first maypole dance. After that we'll have a short welcoming speech, then more dances, then the pageant."

"I don't think I — "

"Nonsense!" Fiona exclaimed. "Of course you can. It's really quite simple, you know, rather like 'London Bridge is falling down.' A child of three could do it."

Fiona seemed determined not to leave Pamela any graceful way out. She looked at Matt, who gave her an apologetic shrug as if to say, "What can we do?" As she followed the tiny English girl toward the maypole, with Matt just behind her, her reluctance began to fade. If ever there was a dancing day, this was it, and if she stepped aside and let it pass her by, she might regret it for a long time.

Fiona placed them facing each other on the edge of the circle and handed each of them a ribbon. Pamela's was bright red, and Matt's was green.

"You keep the ribbon taut with your inner hand and hold the excess in your outer hand," Fiona explained. She took Pamela's hands in her own and demonstrated, then moved on to the next pair of dancers and said the same thing. Pamela looked around. All the ribbons except two on the other side of the circle were taken, but just as she noticed, two people stepped forward and picked them up. She blinked and caught her breath. One of the newcomers was Ben, the other Elise. Ben turned his head and looked straight at her. For a moment she met his eyes, then looked away.

He had known exactly where she was standing. Maybe she was even the reason he had decided to join the dance. The thought, like the sight of him, made her stomach feel as taut and hollow as a drum. But no, she must be mistaken. He was dancing with Elise, the girl he was going out with. Well, he had a right. Wasn't she herself standing there with Matt? Ben was part of a couple and so was she. What happened on the trail, what happened at Laurie's, what had been happening constantly since orientation day, was just an accident. It didn't mean a thing.

Fiona was explaining the dance for the second time. Apparently the men went around the pole in one direction and the women in the other. That sounded easy enough, except that not all the pairs were mixed. Fiona spent a couple of minutes making people honorary males or females, then continued her explanation. Pamela was to go under the ribbon of the first man she met, then the next man was to go under *her* ribbon, and so on. Simple. But when Fiona tried to walk them through it, everyone got totally confused.

Laughing, they disentangled themselves and tried again. It went better, and after the third try Fiona declared that they were ready to try with music. The three musicians standing next to the maypole began to play a lively, bouncy tune that made Pamela feel like skipping. She smiled at Matt as she ducked under his ribbon, then continued to smile as the next man in the circle ducked under hers. Around they went, weaving back and forth, ducking down, then stretching up to clear the next person's head.

Suddenly she came face to face with Ben. His eyes searched her face with an intensity that made her smile flicker for one instant, but then it returned full force. Of course she was meeting him. Like her, he was part of the dance. He hesitated before bowing his head to go under her ribbon. Then they were moving away from each other, but she knew that each step that parted them only brought their next meeting closer.

On the next circuit, it was her turn to put everything she was feeling into her glance. As if by accident, he passed so close to her that their arms and hands brushed. The rush of feeling left her dizzy and confused. She somehow kept herself from falling, then turned in the right direction and ducked under the next ribbon. And still the music played, as jolly and bouncy as ever.

By the end of the dance, half the maypole was hidden under the braided ribbons. Then they had to retrace their steps and *un*braid the ribbons. After a lot of laughter and mass confusion, the ribbons were stretched out and tied to their stakes again. The dancers joined the circle of spectators in clapping and cheering.

As the applause died down, Fiona stepped forward and began to speak. She welcomed everyone to the Revel, thanked the mayor and the Park Service for their cooperation, acknowledged the generous support of so many people and businesses in Rose Hill, and expressed the hope that this would be the first of a long line of annual events.

Pamela shrugged and started to edge toward

the back of the crowd. Fiona sounded as if she were at the start of the commencement address. She was doing it very professionally, but Pamela had little interest in hearing which merchant gave what to the Revel. She was much more interested in the state of her own emotions. She felt like a soda bottle that had been shaken and shaken. The top was still on, so nothing showed, but inside the pressure was growing. At some point very soon she might suddenly begin to bubble and fizz. She'd better — if not, she might explode.

Fiona was starting to talk about the history of maypoles and maypole dancing and their place in the calendar. It sounded like pretty much the same speech Pamela had heard her give three or four times before, when she was recruiting people to help with the Revel. Listening with half an ear, she wandered through the crowd, not knowing where she was going or what she was looking for. Then she was face-to-face with Ben, and the answers became clear.

"Midsummer has a very special place in the cycle of the year," Fiona was saying. "The longest day in all the year — how could it not be special? So a tradition grew up that on Midsummer Day people are entitled to get a little wild, to do things that are unexpected, out of character, even daring. And afterward no one can criticize them for acting a bit crazy, because after all, it was not they who did it. It was the Midsummer madness."

Pamela felt a strange stillness inside her as she

looked at Ben's face. It was such a sweet face, she hated to see the unhappiness and doubt that marred it. Slowly her lips curved into a smile, and to her delight, his expression began to echo hers. Without thinking she moved closer to him, then closer still, and reached out to wrap her arms around his waist. She felt his arms encircling her, and for one searing moment their lips met. Then she realized that they were standing in the middle of a crowd of hundreds of people. She pulled away from his kiss, but she couldn't force herself to let him go. He was just as unable. Still holding each other, they listened to Fiona, then to a medley of English country dances played by the little band, though later on, neither of them could remember what Fiona had said or what the tunes had sounded like.

Finally Ben looked down and met her eyes again. Raising both eyebrows, he motioned with his head toward the back of the crowd. Pamela nodded slowly. She followed him through the circle of merrymakers, then walked by his side down the hill, away from the maypole. As they reached the shelter of the trees, she reached for his arm and placed it around her shoulders again.

Fiona listened to the medley of old-fashioned tunes with a smile on her face, but behind her smile she was thinking at a furious pace. Pamela and Ben? It didn't seem possible. But she knew what she had seen. The way they had looked at each other during the dance, and the way they had sought each other out afterward was unmistakable. She had seen them leave together, too, and she had seen Matt watching them from the crowd.

She shook her head. It was just as she had said — Midsummer madness. It was sure to pass. Pamela and Matt were too well matched, whatever they might think, to split up like that. And although she didn't know Ben and Elise as well, she did know that they had been friends all their lives. They would never let the lure of someone new drive them apart. No one could be so utterly stupid.

It was time to get another dance going, one that would involve more people.

She stepped back into the center of the circle. "Will everyone please go over to one of the ribbons," she said in a loud voice. "For this dance, we shall need two people to each ribbon, so if you haven't a partner, look around and find a likely person."

The milling about that followed was part of the fun. People basically liked to be with each other — all you had to do was find a way to get them to let down their guard. She looked around the circle, smiling at some of the improbable pairings: an elderly woman and a tiny child, two boys who were giggling and poking each other, a man who looked like a lawyer and a girl with pink and green streaks in her hair. And another: Matt and Elise. She watched them for a moment. They were both holding the same ribbon, of course, and it seemed to her that their hands were overlapping. She would have liked to give that some thought, but this wasn't the time. She had a dance to teach.

After five minutes of hard work for her and confusion for practically everybody else, she nodded to the band and the dance began. When the circle came around, she saw that Matt now had his arm around Elise's waist. Her expression confirmed that she wanted it there.

Chapter 25

"Dad, I'm leaving now," Elise said from the doorway to the living room.

"All right, have fun," her father replied, looking up from the Sunday paper. "Will you be home for dinner? I'm going to try my hand at making curry."

"I'll be back before then, but I can't stay to eat. I'm going over to the hospital tonight." She was glad for the excuse. Her father's experiments in cooking were sometimes deliciously successful, but more often they were not.

"Oh. All right, you and Ben have a good time this afternoon."

"It isn't Ben, Daddy. I told you, I'm going for a drive with Matt Jacobs. Oops, here he is — gotta run."

The top was down on the battered Mustang.

As she came out the door, Matt lifted himself up onto the back of his seat and waved. She smiled and waved back. As she crossed the lawn, she couldn't help taking a quick look across the street at Ben's house. She was sure he was home. This was the afternoon he had invited the gang over for a backyard barbecue. Strange — she had been hoping the event would give the two of them a chance to fix their problems. Their problems had gotten fixed, all right, but not at all the way she had expected.

Was he watching from one of those windows, peeping from behind a curtain? She hoped so. She wanted him to see her drive off with Matt. Why should he think he was the only one who was attractive to other people?

"Hi," Matt said as she climbed into the car. He leaned forward to kiss her. A sudden moment of shyness made her turn and lower her head, so that the kiss landed somewhere just above her ear.

"Hi," she replied, settling back in her seat. The upholstery was ripped, and something sharp was jabbing her in the back. She pretended not to notice. She was about to say what a nice day it was, but he blipped the throttle and couldn't have heard her over the noise of the engine.

At the first traffic light, he looked over and said, "Is it too windy for you? There's a scarf in the glove compartment."

"Thanks." The scarf was nothing special, just a green cotton bandanna, but as she was folding it into a triangle, she noticed several spots of paint on it. She tried to tell herself that Matt must have wiped his hands on it while painting something, but she knew better. It was obviously Pamela's. She felt a superstitious fear of putting it on. She was even tempted to let the breeze whisk it away, but she couldn't. Such an act would admit too much. She folded it very small and stuffed it back in the glove compartment. Her hair would have to take care of itself.

A few miles outside of town, Matt turned off the highway onto a road Elise didn't know. It took them through rolling countryside where patches of woods alternated with blooming meadows. Once they passed a new town house development, but most of the houses she saw looked old and well cared for. "Where are we going?" she asked.

He flashed a smile. "It's a surprise. Something a guy told me about the other day that sounded worth taking a look at."

"Oh." She sat back, content simply to be with him and to let him carry her along to some place that he liked. Then she recalled her appointment later. "Is it far?" she said. "I did tell you I have to be back by four-thirty, didn't I?"

"Sure, no sweat. We're practically there."

While he drove, she studied him. His rugged good looks were such a contrast to Ben's friendly, lost-boy looks. Matt had rugged features and dark, intense eyes. In fact, his intensity made him seem just a bit untouchable. Elise wondered if that hands-off quality was part of what she found so attractive in him. It certainly made being with him more unpredictable and more exciting. Ben, on the other hand, was about as predictable as anyone could be.

"That's it," Matt said suddenly, pulling up on the side of the road. They were at the top of a hill overlooking the river. The road wound down the hillside and came to an abrupt end at a rickety-looking wooden dock. From a similar dock on the opposite bank, a strange-looking craft, more like a barge than a boat, was just setting out.

"We're lucky we came on a Sunday," Matt said. "My friend told me that on weekdays commuters have to line up and wait a long time."

"It's a ferryboat," said Elise, then blushed. Had she sounded impossibly dumb? "I didn't know there were any left," she explained.

"There aren't very many. And this one is really unusual."

For a couple of minutes they watched the little boat make its way across the river. Then Matt turned and looked at her with those dark, intense eyes. She found herself leaning toward him, just as he was leaning toward her. Was there really such a thing as a magnetic attraction between two people? The minute she was wrapped in his arms, she stopped wondering. She knew there *was* such a thing. Their kiss seemed to go on and on and it was just as she had imagined it would be. Behind Matt's gruff outer shell, there was an incredible tenderness, and the gentle way he touched her made her dizzy with emotion.

A horn tooted a few feet away from them. Elise opened her eyes and sat up. A car had just edged past them, and another was coming up the road right behind it. Where had they come from?

"Uh-oh," Matt said. "There goes the ferry."

"We missed it?" She felt horribly disappointed and guilty. Matt had driven her all this way just to ride on that ferry, and now they had missed it.

"Don't worry, it'll be back. But we'll have to wait an extra ten or fifteen minutes."

Feeling very daring, Elise smiled at him and said, "That's okay. I bet we can find some way to pass the time."

He narrowed his eyes, then reached for her again.

An eternity later, they started down the hill. At the foot, the road narrowed to a scant two lanes between high, overgrown banks that made it feel almost like a tunnel. Beyond was nothing but water and the other bank. Matt drove onto the dock just as the boat drew closer and began to slow down. Now she could see that the ferry was somehow connected to a cable that stretched across the river from one bank to the other.

"Did you ever ski?" Matt asked.

The ferry nosed up to the dock, which shook alarmingly from the impact. Elise looked over at Matt, but he didn't even seem to notice. "Ski?" she repeated. "Sure, a few times. "Why?"

"The cable. This ferry works on the same principle as a ski lift. It's pulled along by the cable."

Elise nodded.

A couple of cars drove off, then the man on the dock motioned Matt forward. There was a sort of lurch as they drove onto the ferry, and Elise wondered whether anything so obviously obsolete could possibly be safe. Just when she was sure that Matt was going to drive right into the river, he set the brake, shut off the engine, and said, "Let's get out and look around."

After a few minutes of conversation with the man who ran the machinery, he joined her at the railing. She was enchanted. There were no houses in sight, only the river and the wooded hills on either side. Even the road seemed to have lost itself among the trees. The only sounds were the cries of birds and the slap of water against the hull. Then the machinery started up, and they began to glide across the river. The motion itself was strange, more like being pulled than pushed.

"You're right," she said softly, moving closer to Matt and resting her head lightly on his shoulder. "This is a wonderful place. It's so romantic. Why, if we'd been living a hundred years ago, we could have come here, and it would all have been just the same."

He slipped his arm around her. "It's amazing, isn't it? Of course a hundred years ago they would have had a steam engine pulling the cable instead of a diesel. And before that I guess they would have used a team of horses."

She glanced up at him, then smiled to herself. She didn't care whether he wanted to talk about steam engines or solid geometry. He had brought her to this lovely spot, and that was enough. She would always remember it and the warmth of his arms around her and the sweetness of his kiss. She raised her head and gazed into his eyes with a kind of wonder. Then his lips were brushing hers once more, firmly, yet gently, and this time she wanted it to last forever. When she felt the floor shake under her feet, she knew that she had never been kissed like that before.

She opened her eyes. The ferry had completed the crossing and was docked at the other side. Reluctantly she let go of Matt and got into the car, expecting him to turn around and take the ferryboat back across. Instead he drove south, then eastward on a series of narrow country roads. She thought it was a very roundabout route, but he seemed to know where he was going. She sat back and let the sunlight and the breeze envelop her.

Had she dozed off? She wasn't sure. All she knew was that the hands of her watch had moved more than she expected. "Matt?" she said. "I'm not going to be late, am I?"

"Don't worry," he said, keeping his eyes on the road. "I'll get you home in plenty of time. We're just ten or fifteen minutes away from Rose Hill."

She looked around. They were in the midst of rolling farm land, without a house in sight. Could they really be so close to town? It was hard to believe.

The road curved around the base of a hill, then rose to cross between that hill and the next. They were about halfway up the slope when the sound of the engine changed abruptly and the car began to lose speed. Matt muttered under his breath and started to grope around on the floor with his feet. Whatever he was looking for, he apparently didn't find it. The car slowed down to a walk, then a crawl, then stopped. As it started to roll back down the hill, Matt jerked up on the parking brake.

Elise spoke into the sudden silence. "What's the matter?"

"It must be the throttle linkage. I'll have to look to make sure." He got out and opened the hood. A couple of minutes later, he came around to her side and opened the door. She thought he wanted her to get out for some reason, but what he really wanted was the toolbox on the floor behind her.

"Is it what you thought?"

He looked at her as though he had forgotten she was there. "Um? Oh — yeah, it's the throttle linkage. A little piece of it broke right off. Now what can I patch it with?" He began to paw through the toolbox, stopping now and then to look at odd bits of metal.

She looked around at the deserted road and the empty countryside and felt the first tendrils of anxiety brush her lightly.

She cleared her throat. "Um, Matt, how long will it take you to fix it?"

He focused his eyes on her again. "I don't know," he said with a shrug. "If I find something I can use, not too long. If not, we could be stuck here awhile. The nearest house is probably a hefty walk from here, and you don't get that many cars on a road like this. Let's hope we don't have to spend the night."

"The night!" she said. She imagined poor Virginia Coggins watching the clock at the hospital and waiting hopelessly. "Spend the night!" she repeated, even louder. "Matt, I can't spend the night here! I have to go see Tiffany in the hospital tonight!"

He looked at her in amazement, then his face reddened. "Elise, relax, I'm doing what I can."

She huddled in her seat and examined all the dimensions of her misery. She was going to disappoint Tiffany and cause her parents anxiety. It wasn't her fault, but it was the fact that mattered, not who was to blame. And Ben. She was beginning to realize she had lost Ben — or he had lost her, it didn't matter which — not only as the boy she loved, but as her best and oldest friend. That was a heavy loss. And now her own paranoia had just totally blown a new and promising relationship with Matt.

The hood slammed shut. She opened her eyes as Matt vaulted over the side of the car into his seat.

"I fixed it," he said. "You'll still be home by four-thirty."

"Matt, I — "

"It's okay, Elise. I understand, It's a scary thought to be stuck out here all alone. After all, we don't know each other very well yet, do we?"

She reached across and took his hand. "We can get to know each other better," she said softly. "I'd like that."

He patted her hand, then leaned over and gave her a long, sweet kiss that made her feel like she was floating somewhere high above the ground. "So would I. But if I don't get you back on time, you may never speak to me again — or go to the South of the Border amusement park with me on Saturday. And I wouldn't like that at all."

"Oh, Matt! We're going? Really?"

Yep. The Einersons have it all arranged." He looked at her tenderly. "Now, let's get going," he said, smiling. "Friends again?"

"Friends," Elise replied. And she meant it.

Dick decided to take a short run. He had packed up the night before, so he hadn't anything else to do.

A good, brisk run will help me think, he told himself. He began to trot away from the campgrounds, along the row of tall trees that lined the path. The air was cool and crisp. The sun dappled the ground with shifting shadows.

Car after car pulled up the path, parents arriving to take their computer geniuses home.

Some genius I turned out to be, he thought. But then he forced all thoughts of the competition from his mind. He had plenty of other things to think about.

What a crazy two weeks!

He had ridden all the way to Maine thinking about Laurie. And now he was about to ride home, thinking about how he was going to break up with Laurie.

He had never been in a spot like this in his life. Everyone knew that Dick Westergard was steady as a rock, a loyal friend, not fickle, not moody, sensitive but not overly emotional.

Of all the crazy things!

But maybe, he thought, that's what the real thing is when it hits you. Crazy.

And he was sure this was the real thing with Roxanne.

Well . . . he was pretty sure.

Some of Frankie's remarks suddenly found their way into his mind as he picked up his pace, turned, and began to run back toward the camp. He remembered some of Frankie's jokes about how boy-crazy Rox was and how she collected boys as a hobby.

But this was different, Dick thought. This had to be different. Why was he even thinking these things about her? What was going on?

Enough. Enough running. And enough thinking. For a while, anyway. He knew he had to think about how he was going to break up with Laurie, what he could say to her that would make any sense. But he had the whole ride back to think about that.

He waved as Frankie and Roxanne rode off with Frankie's parents. But they must not have seen him, because they didn't wave back.

He trotted up to the yellow mansion and sat down on the lowest step. He could see all the way down the hill from here, and far beyond the camp. There were no cars on the road. He was going back on the van, later that day.

He thought about going into the game room and getting a cold soda. But then he realized he didn't really have the energy to climb all those steps. He decided to sit right there and wait the couple hours till the van arrived.

From time to time Pamela looked up and caught one of the gang giving her a funny look. She knew why. All these kids on Everett Street had known each other for years. They had walked to school together every morning and played together every afternoon and shared snowball fights and skateboard races and backyard cookouts like this one for as long as they could remember. She was the newcomer, the outsider, who was there only because Ben had asked her, and it was his party.

As if being the outsider at the party weren't bad enough, some girl who couldn't have been more than fourteen had practically glued herself to Ben. At the moment he was trying to put a batch of franks on the grill, and she was trying to tickle his neck with a blade of grass. She had to stand on tiptoe to reach, and to keep her balance she was also leaning against him.

"Come on, Dora, cut it out," he said, but he was too late. The grass blade must have touched a sensitive spot. The tongs in his hand gave a convulsive jerk and a frankfurter went sailing end over end across the yard. Wolfie, a German shepherd that belonged to one of the gang, woke up, made a running leap, and caught the frank in midair. Some people started clapping, but Ben looked mad. "Now I'm going to have too many buns and not enough franks," he complained.

"Throw Wolfie a bun," someone suggested.

"Yeah," another added, "and don't forget the mustard and onions."

A guy whose name Pamela thought was Gary said, "Remember the time Wolfie took off after Sharon's cat?"

"That was such a riot," a blonde girl with huge sunglasses said, then turned to the girl next to her and added, "I swear, I nearly died. The cat ran through the flowerbed and then jumped right onto Elise's lap. She was wearing that yellow sundress of hers, and the cat got mud all over it."

Gary guffawed. "That wasn't anything compared to what Wolfie did to it when he tried to follow the cat onto her lap. But Ben came to the rescue, right, fella?"

Ben grinned and pointed to his left forearm. "I've still got the scars," he said. "That's when I learned that cats have sharper claws than dogs."

Unable to participate in the conversation, Pamela turned and walked across the yard, away from the others, and sat down on the grass behind a tree. She hadn't done it deliberately to get Ben away from the others, but when she heard his footsteps, she realized how much she had hoped he would notice her leave and follow her.

"Are you okay?" he said, kneeling down next to her.

"No." She took the hem of her skirt and began to pleat it with her fingers.

"Oh." A pause. "It's too bad the other counselors couldn't make it this afternoon. I guess I should have thought of asking them sooner."

"It doesn't matter. Except for Erin, I don't really know any of them that well."

"Yeah, same here. You'll like these kids once you get to know them, though. They're a terrific bunch."

She didn't reply. He was probably right, but it didn't change her sense of being left out.

"I know it's tough on you ,but you've got to meet some of my friends. Besides" — he smiled — "we'll have a night out with the gang on Saturday at South of the Border. That should cheer you up."

Only if Matt's not there, Pamela thought. But

she smiled warmly at Ben. “Come on,” she said, getting to her feet and helping to pull him up. “We’d better get back to the party.”

Once he was up, he took her shoulders, pressed her back against the tree, and began to kiss her. For a few seconds she let herself enjoy it, but then she pushed him away and wriggled free. She was sure that his friends must be watching and talking among themselves. Did they all hate her for taking Elise’s place?

Chapter 26

A few moments later, he heard footsteps behind him. He turned around to see Bill Willard coming down the steps, suitcase in hand.

"Hey, Westergard — how come you're always last?" Willard called cheerily. "Last to leave the computer lab, and last to leave the camp."

"Guess I'm just slow," Dick told him. Seeing Willard reminded Dick that he had just lost the competition. With everything else on his mind, he hadn't thought about it for a while.

Willard shook his hand. "Guess this is goodbye," he said. He waved to someone in a red Pontiac down on the road. "I'm cutting out to the Staunton diner before the next group starts arriving. It was nice having you here."

"Thanks. I had fun," Dick said, somewhat less enthusiastically than he should have.

"You had a really good start on that word game of yours," Willard said. "But there were just too many bugs in the program."

Dick looked up at him as if he weren't speaking English. "Word game? What word game?"

"You know. Jumble Word. Isn't that what you called the word game program you entered in the competition? It was a clever idea, but you just didn't follow through."

"Word game? *What*?" Dick was in shock.

The person in the red Pontiac honked the horn.

"Coming!" Willard yelled. But the horn honked again. "Listen, Dick. I've gotta go."

"Just one second. Please," Dick said, climbing to his feet. "There's some kind of mistake, Bill."

Willard waved to the car. "Really. I've got to get going," he told Dick impatiently. "What are you saying? What kind of mistake?"

"I didn't do a word game," Dick told him. His mind was whirring in confusion. What on earth was Willard talking about? Had there been some major mix-up or something?

"Yes. Word Jumble. Your name was at the top. There was only one Dick Westergard at camp, right?"

"But, Bill — " Dick said, trying to keep his voice calm and steady. "I didn't do a word game. I did a program for real estate offices, something to help them keep track of their listings."

"That was Roxanne's program," Willard said, giving him an odd look. "That's the program she won with. Very clever. Very complicated, but it all worked." He paused for a second. "Hey — are you feeling all right?"

Dick didn't answer.

"Westergard — are you okay?"

The horn honked. "I'm coming!" Willard yelled.

"Oh. Uh . . . yeah. Fine. I'm fine," Dick said. " 'Bye, Bill. Have a good year."

"Yeah. You, too." Willard hurried off to the waiting car.

Dick sat back down on the step and stared straight ahead until the car became a red blur. The car was a blur, but everything else was coming clear for him.

"I can't believe it," he said aloud. "What a snake! I just kissed her good-bye. I promised to break up with Laurie for her! And all the while she knew the trick she had played on me."

Why had she done it? It was pretty easy to figure out. To get back at him for rejecting her. She had been toying with him the whole while. He was another prize to add to her collection. And he had fallen for it, fallen for her, fallen for everything!

Frankie had tried to warn him, but he had been too blind, too hypnotized by those dazzling green eyes, by her movie-star looks, her whisper of a voice.

Roxanne Easton had claimed another victim.

Well . . . yes and no.

He was wise to her now. At least he wouldn't continue to make a complete and utter fool of himself when he got back to Rose Hill. At least he wouldn't give Roxanne the opportunity to laugh at him again, to play him for the fool — the fool that he was!

He jumped to his feet and, still shaking his head, trotted quickly up the steps, and pushed open the front door to the house. He went straight to the phone booth in the game room, searched his jeans pocket for all the change he had, and with a shaking hand, dialed a familiar phone number.

He let it ring till he couldn't stand it any longer. Laurie wasn't home.

At the edge of the sand, Laurie knelt down to adjust the laces of her new Nikes. They only came in one color, a shade of lavender that made her skin look sallow, and the way the heel bulged out under her foot was particularly clunky, but she felt proud of them. What did fashion matter? These were top-of-the-line running shoes, orthopedically designed, practically guaranteed to add miles to her range. That's what the shoe salesman at Superjock had said, anyway.

He had tried to get her to buy a pair of over-the-top-of-the-line shoes, shiny silver Gore-Tex with a built-in microchip that kept track of how far and how fast she ran. She was tempted, but they seemed a little, well, ostentatious. A wealthy lawyer who was just taking up jogging might buy them, but not a serious runner like she was. Besides, she had just bought a red and white watch on a red lanyard that not only tracked her time and distance but had a little running figure on the face that gave her the pace she wanted.

She finished tightening her laces, straightened up, and checked her wristwatch. The new lanyard watch was back on her dresser, gathering dust. True, her wristwatch didn't have a little running figure that paced her, but it didn't bump into the same spot on her stomach at every step, either. The time was just past seven-thirty. If Rick was following his usual schedule, he ought to come into view at any moment. She trotted across the beach to near the water and began to warm up.

She was seated with one leg tucked under her and the other stretched out straight, trying to touch her head to her knee, when Rick ran up and said, "Hi. Nice day for a run, isn't it?"

He had said that every morning for over a week, including the morning on which a front out of Canada brought them a chilly, drenching rain. Was it just habit, or did he really believe that every day was a nice day for a run?

Today, however, she happened to agree with him. "It sure is," she said, giving him a brilliant smile. She leaned back on her hands, straightened her legs, and made a bridge, then let herself down and reached to clasp her toes. Her calves still needed a lot of work.

"Ready? How about an easy five miles?"

She groaned inwardly. She was gaining stamina every day, but she wasn't ready for five miles, easy or not. "Why don't we do three," she said, "then break for a swim, then three more? Wouldn't that be more like a triathlon?"

He shrugged, and all the muscles in his chest and shoulders rippled and gleamed. He apparently noticed the effect and liked it, because he did it again. "Whatever," he said. "I'm going to put in another six or eight before lunch anyway. How about a bike ride this afternoon?"

"No, thanks." She had made *that* mistake once already. His idea of a bike ride was going full speed for ten or fifteen miles, turning around, and coming back at the same speed. The only way she had survived the ride was by dropping out, taking a long rest, and letting him catch her on the way home. Even so, and in spite of a lambskin cover on her bicycle seat, she had come home with raw spots on the inside of her thighs that were only now healing. "I'm leaving after lunch. I've got to go back to town for a couple of days."

"Oh. Too bad. Ready?"

She was beginning to understand why people liked to run. It wasn't just the act of moving, but something about using the body the way it was meant to be used. The first two miles went by quickly. During the third she started to tire out, but it comforted her to know that if she had to she could probably keep going even farther.

As usual, they ran in an unbroken silence. Why was it that the people who were in good enough condition to carry on a conversation while running were the same people who never had anything to say? No question, Rick was a charter member of the club. Even when he was standing still, he usually spoke in short sentences and words of one or two syllables. Once he began to move, his entire mind seemed to focus itself on what his muscles were doing. She doubted if he even thought about anything else; he didn't talk about anything at all. She certainly wasn't that way. She always thought of plenty of things to say as she was running along the beach, but she never had enough breath left over to say them.

She glanced over at him. She loved to look at him, to see how effortlessly his body worked, but his lack of interest in looking at her had become a major irritation. She was used to getting a good deal of attention and admiration for her looks, and he wasn't contributing anything like his proper share. Most of the time he didn't seem to notice her at all.

"The breakwater is about three miles," he said.

"Great," she gasped, eyeing the distance that remained.

At the breakwater he dropped his running shoes on the sand and dived into the surf. After swimming out fifty yards or so, he turned south and churned the water as if he were late for a lunch date in Miami. Laurie watched him go, then waded in and played in the breakers. As she bobbed up and down, she asked herself for the dozenth time why she was working so hard at attracting Rick. It *was* hard work, too. When she managed to get him over to the house three nights before, he hadn't even noticed the candles, the plates of interesting snacks, her new outfit, or the stack of the latest music videos by the VCR. All he wanted to do was eat carrots and talk about his practice times. The only guaranteed way to hold his attention would be to go around with a big mirror strapped to her chest. *Then* he'd look at her.

The truth was, her whole summer was going down the tubes, and she was standing by and letting it happen. The idea of spending six weeks at the beach house had sounded great, but the reality was somewhere between boredom and utter depression. She always liked to have a lot of friends around her, and out here she didn't have any at all. The party had been terrific, but it had only lasted one afternoon and evening. Then everyone else went back to Rose Hill and left her alone again. The only person she ever saw was Rick, and since he didn't talk, she didn't talk to anyone at all.

The person she wanted to see and talk to was Dick Westergard. She really missed him. There, she had finally admitted it.

Oh, sure, she had been furious at him for going to Maine for that job at the computer camp and abandoning her for most of the summer. She was still furious, more or less. But she had managed to convince herself that anger was *all* she felt, and that was a lie. She had a lot of other feelings, too: hurt that he could go so easily, sadness that they would miss sharing the whole summer together before college, regret that she hadn't really shown him how deeply she cared about him, and above all, a wrenching loneliness. Maybe that was one of her reasons for taking up running — to wear herself out so completely that she went to bed exhausted and didn't lie awake missing him.

Maybe she should call him at camp again. But what if he wasn't free when she called, or what if he didn't want to talk to her? Well, he would probably get the message she had called, and at least he would know that she wanted to reach him.

Once the idea hit her, she was almost sick with impatience to carry it out. She waded ashore and turned to scan the water. Rick was nowhere in sight. Maybe he *had* decided to swim to Florida. She didn't have any way to leave him a message, but it didn't much matter. When he did come back, he would probably notice that she wasn't there and decide that she must have left. She walked up the beach a few yards to let the warm sand dry her feet, then put on her special running socks and professional-caliber running shoes. She was about to set a personal record for the three-mile run.

The man who answered the phone at the camp said he would go look for Dick. It wasn't more than a minute or so later that she heard Dick's voice say, "Laurie?" He sounded almost as out of breath as she was.

"Hi, Dick."

"Oh, Laurie, I've missed you so much."

She closed her eyes and gripped the telephone

so tightly her knuckles ached. "I've missed you, too," she said softly.

"I have so much to tell you." Dick's voice was so low that Laurie could hardly hear him.

"Oh, Dick. I have a lot to tell you, too."

"Listen, is there any way you can get up here for a few days? The course is over, but I can get permission to stay until the next group of kids arrives."

"Why, I — " Her mind raced. She would need her father's okay, but she didn't think he would refuse it. He and Dick got along very well. "I'd love to," she said. "I really want to see you. But what could I do up there? I don't know a thing about computers."

"That's perfect. I don't even want to think about computers right now. Plus, it's a gorgeous place with beaches — wi . . . with miles of trails."

"Trails?" she said, puzzled. "For horses, you mean?"

"I haven't had a chance to tell you, but since I came up here, I've found a new interest." Laurie heard his voice catch slightly. "What I mean is, I've taken up cross-country running. You've got to try it; it's great fun."

Oh, no! she said to herself, rolling her eyes. But to Dick she said, "I'll bet it is. I can hardly wait."

Chapter 27

Pamela took a bite of her cheese enchilada, then went back to playing with the refried beans with her fork. She usually liked Mexican food, but right now she didn't have much of an appetite.

All afternoon at the South of the Border amusement park, she and Ben and the other kids from Rose Hill had sampled such attractions as the Aztec Temple (a haunted house with feathered robes and human sacrifices), Under the Volcano (a roller coaster inside a fake mountain), and the Acapulco Water Slide (a water slide). Even the merry-go-round featured burros instead of horses.

The most unbelievable, though, was a ride called La Cucaracha. The little cars that zipped around a twisty track were shaped like cockroaches. Pamela and Ben had watched it awe-struck for a couple of minutes, then Ben looked around and asked loudly if there was an exterminator in the place. The man in the ticket booth had looked ready to kill, but as Pamela pointed out, he probably heard comments like that fifty times a day.

For dinner the Einersons had reserved a private dining room with half a dozen tables and a fine view of the fake volcano. Diana and Jeremy took the head table, of course, along with her parents, Bart, and Bart's girl friend, Holly. The rest of the guests were free to sit where they liked. This led to a good deal of shuffling and dickering as people tried to end up at the same table as their friends without insulting everybody else.

At a certain point Pamela had gotten fed up with the entire process and led Ben over to a table that was still empty. They reached it at the exact moment that Matt and Elise approached from the other direction. The two couples had been carefully keeping out of each other's way all afternoon, though they could hardly avoid exchanging meaningful glances from time to time. Pamela couldn't hide the bitterness she had been feeling ever since the moment Matt had stepped onto the bus with Elise. What had become of that all-important job at the gas station? Why was he able to get time off to be with Elise, when he couldn't for her?

They stood around the table, their faces reddening, for what seemed like forever. Finally Ben took a step backward, but as if that were a sign,

Elise muttered something that might have been an apology and turned away. Matt followed her to another table across the room. The incident left Ben looking utterly depressed, especially after he saw Fiona and Jonathan sit down at Elise and Matt's table. But then Dee and her boyfriend, Marc, came over and sat down, and Ben seemed to cheer up a little. A few moments later the two remaining seats were taken by Colin Edwards, whom Ben apparently knew from science classes and the Computer Club, and a girl named Amy. And almost immediately after that, waitresses wearing colorful aprons and immense sombreros had arrived with their dinners.

"Aren't you hungry?" Ben asked.

"Not really," Pamela replied.

"You don't like Mexican food, huh?"

"Yes, I do," she said. "I've just kind of lost my appetite."

For a moment he looked concerned, then Colin asked him a question about some new software the Computer Club had bought in the spring, and he turned away.

From across the table, Dee said, "Are you getting a lot of painting done this summer?"

"Not as much as I'd like," Pamela answered. "I'm working full-time at a day camp until the end of July."

"Yeah. It's tough having a job and keeping up with your own interests, too," said Dee. "When I get home from work, all I do is eat dinner, watch some TV, and go to bed. The last thing I want to do is to put in three or four hours of darkroom time. I still haven't developed my shots from Laurie's beach party, and I've got four or five rolls from the Midsummer Revel sitting there, too. I hardly have time to stay in shape!"

"Dee doesn't go to parties anymore," Marc said, "she just photographs them."

Pamela laughed, but the remark left her feeling uncomfortable. Was Marc saying that Dee's passion for photography was getting in the way of their relationship?

Matt had sometimes acted jealous of the amount of time Pamela spent on her art, but he had also been proud of her work. He had seen the effort and dedication that she put into it, and he had admired her for it. He knew about those qualities, because he needed them himself to carry out his self-chosen task of rescuing interesting cars from the scrap heap.

Pamela frowned and shifted uncomfortably in her seat. She had resented Matt's involvement with the Mustang because she felt the time he spent on it, the time he spent working to pay for it, was time taken away from her. But wasn't that just what Marc was saying to Dee? What if Matt had told her not to paint so much because it was interfering with their social life? She would have thought that was incredibly crass and insensitive of him. Wasn't she being just as crass and insensitive about his interest in cars?

While she was still pondering this question, the waitresses in their sombreros began to clear the tables. Bart stood up and tapped his fork on his glass.

"Speech!" someone shouted.

Bart grinned and held up his hands for silence. "It's a known fact that speechifying runs in my family," he said, glancing at his congressman father, "but you're going to be spared this time. I just want to make sure everybody knows the program. Now in ten minutes or so we're going to go over to the arena for the concert."

There were hoots and cheers and shouts of "all right."

"Then afterward, we'll come back for cake and ice cream and a chorus of 'Happy Birthday.' " He turned and winked at his sister, who smiled and blushed.

"So if anybody gets separated in the crowd," he concluded, "don't panic. We'll be waiting for you right in this room."

As he sat down to cheerful applause, Ben said, "I can't wait to see the Torrid Twisters in person. I hear they have one of the most advanced sound systems in the world."

"The special effects are supposed to be really amazing, too," Colin said. "The whole show is preprogrammed and run by a thirty-two-bit micro."

Ben looked impressed. Pamela felt depressed. She didn't know anything about thirty-two-bit micros, but she knew one important thing about the band. They played *very loud*. As for a preprogrammed, computer-run show, she couldn't help wondering what would happen if one of the musicians had to stop to scratch an itch. Would the whole rest of the show be out of sync?

She glanced around the room. The others seemed to be very excited about the concert. Maybe she was the one who was out of synch.

Their seats were all together in the center section, just in front of the base of the light tower and about a dozen rows back from the stage. The tall stacks of loudspeakers on either side of the stage seemed close enough to touch, and the skeletal framework of the light tower loomed directly over their heads. Pamela twisted in her seat and looked around. Some of the seats at the very back and at the sides were empty, but lines of people were still filing in. She couldn't even guess how many the arena held — five thousand? More than that? Whatever the number, the Torrid Twisters seemed to be drawing a full house.

Matt and Elise were in the next row back, a few seats to her left. As she was settling back into her seat, she met Matt's gaze. For one instant, he looked at her the old way, the way she had thought he would always look at her. Then, just as she felt herself start to respond to the warmth in his eyes, a steel wall came clanging down, and he was looking at her as if she were a stranger or even an enemy.

She stared down at her clasped hands. She was not going to cry. Later, perhaps, when she was alone in her room, but not here, not now. She had hoped that they would stay friends, even if their days as a couple were numbered. That was beginning to seem like a foolish dream. She didn't know what she could do to smooth things over, but she *did* want him to be glad to see her — not hurt or mad. What *could* she do?

Recorded music began to blast from the speakers, and already a crowd was gathering in front of the stage, swaying and dancing with their arms stretched high, waving their fingers jerkily at the darkening sky. Some of the people around her were getting to their feet, too, though so far there was nothing to see but a bunch of instruments and speakers on an otherwise empty stage.

Ben put his arm around her. She couldn't help glancing back. Matt had his arm around Elise, too. Had the two guys consulted each other by telepathy? Or was there a certain moment that only males were sensitive to, when it was time to put your arm around your date?

Why was she so concerned with what Matt was doing, anyway? Their time as a couple had come to an end. It was Ben's arm around her. Ben who she — Pamela stopped herself. Did she love Ben the way she had loved Matt? She closed her eyes and imagined herself sitting in Elise's place. Suddenly she could almost feel Matt's presence. The intensity of that sensation overwhelmed her.

Suddenly the arena went dark, and a voice boomed, "Ladies and gentlemen, South of the Border is proud to present the newest, hottest rock band. Will you please welcome THE TORRID TWISTERS!"

The crowd went totally bonkers, cheering, whistling, and stomping on their chairs, as the spotlights picked out five fantastic figures who ran out onto the stage and picked up their instruments. One of them, in leather pants, grabbed a microphone from its stand, and shouted, "*Three, four . . . !*"

The crashing chords washed over the arena, pressing the listeners back into their seats with sheer sound pressure. The stage lights and spotlights changed color and intensity unpredictably, now glaring, now dropping to a level where the brightest thing on stage was the afterimage in the spectators' brains. Laser beams, thin as a thread but impossibly intense, whipped across the sky so fast that they didn't seem to move from here to there, but simply to *be* here and then *be* there. Clouds of colored smoke rose from the front of the stage, obscuring the band for a few moments before being dispersed by the breeze.

Pamela tried to get into the music, but she couldn't. At that volume she couldn't make out words or melody, or anything at all except the relentless beat that came to her as much through her chest and the soles of her feet as through her ears. Visually, however, she managed to stay interested for about half the show. After that she grew bored. There were only so many color combinations for the lights and so many ways to run, leap, and prance across the stage. And after the twentieth time of watching laser beams slice through colored smoke, she couldn't have cared less. She sat down, stuck her fingers in her ears, and closed her eyes.

Suddenly she realized that the quality of the screams around her had changed from excitement to terror. She opened her eyes and jumped up. Dazed by the abrupt transition, she needed a moment to figure out what was happening. In that moment, a wave of panicky kids pressed back toward her, trying to escape the column of greasy yellow smoke that was rising from the floor of the arena a few rows ahead.

Ben was gripping her arm and shouting something at her, but she didn't dare listen. There wasn't time. The pressure of the mob was wrenching the seats loose from the floor and toppling both seats and people, who screamed as further waves of terrified fans tripped and crashed down on them. Pamela tried to back away, but her row of seats, still standing for the moment, caught her at the knees and almost brought her down.

She discovered a strange hard-edged clarity to her thoughts. Whatever the cost, she had to stay on her feet. Once down, she would never manage to get up again. Those behind her would trample her. She needed something to give shelter, to divert the stream around her until the flood passed. The only permanent structure in the whole arena was the light tower. In the very instant that she thought of it, she vaulted over the back of her seat, climbed over the next row, and pulled herself up onto the lowest crosspiece of the tower.

The yellow smoke was thinning out, and the screams were dying down, to be replaced by sobs of pain and fright. But just as the panic flight began to ease, there was new danger from the other direction as those far from the scene pressed forward to see what was happening. A booming voice pleaded for people to return to their seats, then threatened that the show would be canceled if they didn't. No one seemed to listen.

Pamela, safe on her perilous perch, was beginning to recover from her own terror, only to realize how many other terrors confronted her. Were her friends safe? Where was Matt? She scanned the faces in the area where he had been sitting, but they were all strangers. Her free hand clutched her throat as she pictured him lying on the concrete floor, kicked and battered. What if he was in a coma, or worse? He would never know how much she loved him.

Pamela blinked fiercely, trying to clear the blurring film from her eyes. She could cry later, after she got out of this horrible place. Right now she had to *know*. Slowly, carefully, she looked from one sector of the mob to another, searching every face for the one face she ached to see. She saw many of her friends from Kennedy. She saw Ben holding a handkerchief to his cheek, searching frantically through the crowd. Was he looking for her? She wanted to call to him, but he was too far away and the pandemonium was too overpowering. She saw Elise, too, looking lost but determined. They were both all right, then. When Elise crossed Ben's path, and they hugged each other, Pamela felt a tremendous rush of relief. If only things worked out this way when she found Matt. Matt — where was he? Why was his the only face she didn't see anywhere in the crowd?

A hand grabbed her ankle and almost pulled her down. "Pamela!" Matt shouted. "Are you all right?"

When she saw the worry on his face, she reached out with both hands to comfort him. An instant later she fell off the crossbar into his waiting arms.

Everyone wanted to talk at once. Maybe it made the shock more manageable. Everyone had a story to tell, and quite a few had bruises and scrapes to show. Two of their party were absent: Marc had been taken to the local hospital with a broken arm, and Dee had gone along to keep him company.

"I tell you, I saw it," Woody was saying. "I just happened to look over that way, and there was a *phttt!* and this thing the size of a bowling ball went flying up and landed about four rows in front of us. It just missed a girl with a ponytail."

Pamela looked at Matt and knew he was thinking the same thing she was. The girl with the ponytail could have been her, or him, and the defective smoke bomb could have hit instead of missed. Life was not something to take for granted. Neither was love.

"Excuse me a second," Matt said, and walked across the room to where Elise was sitting.

"Pamela?"

Ben had bandages on his cheek and his head had a nasty bump just over one eyebrow.

"Are you all right?" she asked.

"More or less," he said wryly. "I tried to help you when I saw what was happening, but I guess I wasn't even much good at helping myself. And now I've got to say something you'll probably hate me for."

"Ben, I — "

"No, wait. When the crowd started panicking and the seats fell over, I tried to protect us, but all I could really think about was that Elise was in danger, and I wasn't there for her. That's really awful of me, isn't it? I mean, uh . . . I suddenly realized what I should have known all along, that Elise and I — "

She reached up and touched her fingertip to his lips. "I understand, Ben," she said softly. "And I don't hate you or think you're awful. I think you're pretty wonderful."

Impulsively she threw her arms around his neck and kissed him. When she opened her eyes, she found Matt and Elise standing a few feet away, watching. Matt had his arm around Elise.

She took a step backward. Had they misunderstood her kissing Ben like that? Or was she the one who had misunderstood?

Just as her confusion was beginning to turn to doubt, Elise took Matt's hand and gave it to Pamela, then went over to Ben and slipped her arm around his waist. As they walked away, she looked back at Pamela for a long moment. Her expression seemed to say that it was hard to give up something good, even if it was for the sake of something more important. Pamela nodded in agreement. Then she turned to Matt's embrace.

"Pamela?" he said after they shared a long, deep kiss. "I'm going to ask my uncle to put me back on the day shift and not give me so much weekend work."

"Are you sure?" she asked doubtfully. She didn't want him making a decision that he would hold against her later.

"I'm sure. I didn't have my head on straight before. But now I understand what really matters to me, and it isn't a new carb. It's you. It's us. I can keep the old carb working a while longer."

Before she could react, Bart walked to the front of the room and said, "Friends, today has turned out to be a little more memorable than we would have liked. And I know we all have Marc in our thoughts and wish him a quick recovery from his injury. But we shouldn't let what happened this evening make us forget that this is also a celebration. Sis, where are you? Get yourself up here!"

Diana laughed. "That sounds more like the brother I know and love!"

As Diana reached the front of the room, the lights went down and her parents came in carrying a big cake with flaming candles. Everyone began to sing "Happy Birthday."

At least, everyone but Pamela and Matt. As soon as the lights began to dim, Matt had pulled Pamela tenderly into his arms. She gave him a kiss that carried with it all the passion and longing she found she had been storing up for weeks. By the end of it she was breathless and almost faint. When his arms tightened around her, and he pulled her as close as it was possible to get, she knew that she was going to have a wonderful summer after all.

Coming Soon . . .
Couples #24
SOMETHING NEW

Amy walked over to the window, wondering if any of the wedding guests had arrived. She was just in time to see a beat-up silver Chevrolet pull into the wide, circular driveway. It clanked and clattered. Then the driver got out and Amy couldn't keep from gasping. He was simply gorgeous.

The boy stood for a moment, tucking the tails of his yellow oxford shirt into his jeans. His shirt-sleeves were rolled to the elbow, revealing tanned, muscular arms. Amy smiled. This boy was as different from Colin as night was from day.

She was aware of the warmth spreading through her and flushed. She tried to force herself to turn away, but she was rooted to the spot. Without warning, the boy looked up at her.

His ruddy, broad-featured face broke into the

most bewitching smile she'd ever seen. It seemed to pierce her soul. Giddily she hid behind the lace curtain sashed against the window.

Who *was* he? A delivery boy for her cousin Andrea's wedding? No. He wasn't carrying anything. On the other hand, he certainly wasn't dressed to go out to dinner, so he couldn't be one of the guests.

Later, Amy felt her insides go fluttery as she peeked out from behind the curtain and peered down again. A dizzying wave of disappointment flowed through her, and she gripped the windowsill tightly.

The old silver car was still parked where she'd seen it last. But the boy with the bewitching smile was gone. She closed her eyes and told herself she had no right to feel so disappointed. But she couldn't escape the sinking feeling that engulfed her.

by Tina Oaks

Chapter Excerpt

Paige Whitman unzipped the plastic cover that held the dress she was to wear to her father's wedding. She had put off looking at the dress until the very last minute. When she learned the dress would be pink, she had groaned. There were colors she loved, colors she could take or leave alone, and then there was pink, which hated her as much as she hated it!

And the style was as impossible for her as the color. She didn't even have to try the dress on to know how it would look. At sixteen she was taller than most of her friends, and thinner without being really skinny. But taller meant longer, and she knew her neck was too long to wear a low, rounded neckline like that.

Paige's instinct was to wail. Dresses were supposed to do things *for* you, not *to* you. The only tiny comforting thing she could think of was that Katie Summer Guthrie, her fifteen-year-old stepsister-to-be would be wearing a matching monstrosity. Even though pink was a blonde's color, not even Katie could look like anything in *that* dress. It was comforting that she wouldn't be alone in her humiliation.

Beyond the other bed in the hotel room they shared, Paige's ten-year-old sister Megan hummed happily as she put on her own dress. Megan was a naturally happy-go-lucky girl, but Paige had never seen her as excited as she had been since their father announced his coming marriage to Virginia Mae Guthrie. Her father had tried to control his own excitement and tell them about his bride-to-be in a calm, sensible way. But Paige knew him too well to be fooled, and anyway he gave himself dead away!

He started by telling them how he had met Virginia Mae on a business trip to Atlanta, then how beautiful she was. He went from that to her divorce five years before and how she had been raising her three children alone ever since. Paige almost giggled. Here was William Whitman, whose logic and cool courtroom delivery were legendary in Philadelphia legal circles. Yet he was jumping around from one subject to another as he talked about Virginia Mae.

Paige had driven down to Atlanta with her father and Megan earlier in the summer so the children could meet. Paige had to agree that Virginia Mae Guthrie was as lovely as she was gentle.

Paige had tried to shrug away the twinge of resentment that came when she thought of Katie Summer. The girl had to be putting on an act. *Nobody* could possibly be as lighthearted and happy as she pretended to be. And nobody would be that pretty in a fair world. Seventeen-year-old Tucker seemed like a nice enough guy, although his exaggerated good manners threw Paige off a little. Ten-year-old Mary Emily was cute. But it was awkward to be the only one holding back when her father and Megan were both so obviously deliriously happy.

Her father made the marriage plans sound so simple: "Right after our wedding, Virginia and the children will move up here to Philadelphia. We'll all be one big happy family together."

Paige had said nothing then or since, but concealing her doubts hadn't made them go away. She hated feeling like a sixteen-year-old grouch, but it just didn't make sense that everything would work out that easily. Not only would there be more than twice as many people in the same house as before, but the people themselves would be different.

Even if people from the south didn't think differently than people from the north, they certainly *sounded* different when they talked. And the Guthries were as completely southern as Paige's family was northern. Mrs. Guthrie and her three children had lived in Atlanta all their lives.

Megan giggled and fluffed out her full skirt. "Isn't it great? I can't wait to show this dress back home."

Back home. Philadelphia meant only one person to Paige . . . Jake Carson. She shuddered at the thought of Jake seeing her in that pink dress. She would die, just simply die where she stood, if he ever saw her looking this gross.

She sighed and fiddled with the neck of the pink dress, wishing she hadn't even thought of Jake. Simply running his name through her mind was enough to sweep her with those familiar waves of almost physical pain. It didn't make sense that loving anyone could be so painful. But just the memory of his face, his intense expression, the brooding darkness of his thoughtful eyes was enough to destroy her self-control.

But even when Jake looked at her, he was absolutely blind to who she really was. She knew what he thought: that she was a nice kid, that she was fun to talk to, that she was William Whitman's daughter. Period. He didn't give the slightest indication that he even realized that she was a girl, much less a girl who loved him with such an aching passion that she couldn't meet his eyes for fear he might read her feelings there.

Megan caught Paige around the waist and clung to her. "Sometimes I get scared, thinking about the changes. It *is* going to be wonderful, isn't it, Paige?" Megan's voice held the first tremulous note of doubt Paige had heard from her sister.

"Absolutely wonderful," Paige assured her, wishing she felt as much confidence as she put into her tone.

Even as she spoke, she saw Jake's face again, his dark eyes intent on hers as he had talked to her about the wedding. "Look at your dad," Jake had said. "Anything that makes him that happy has to be a lucky break for all of you."

She had nodded, more conscious of how lucky she was to be with Jake than anything else.

Jake had worked around their house in Philadelphia for about a year and a half. Paige didn't believe in love at first sight, but it had almost been that way with her. From the first day, she found herself waiting breathlessly for the next time he came to work. She found herself remembering every word he said to her, turning them over and over in her mind later. It wasn't that he was mysterious. It was more that she always had the sense of there being so much more in his mind than he was saying. She was curious about him, his life, his friends, how he thought about things. In contrast to a lot of people who smiled easily and laughed or hummed when they worked, he was silent and withdrawn unless he was talking with someone.

Before he came, she hadn't realized how painful it was to love someone the way she did Jake. She hadn't asked to fall in love with him or anybody. She had even tried desperately to convince herself that he wasn't different from other boys, just nicer and older. That didn't work because it wasn't true. Jake really was different from the boys she knew at school. Although he talked enough when he had something to say, he was mostly a little aloof without being awkward and shy. And he wasn't an ordinary kind of handsome. His features were strong, with firm cheekbones; deeply set eyes; and a full, serious mouth.

Maybe one day she would quit loving him as quickly as she had begun. But even thinking about that happening brought a quick thump of panic in her chest. Knowing how it felt to be so much in love, how could she bear to live without it?

Later, when the wedding march began and the doors of the little chapel were opened, Paige was overwhelmed with the strange feeling that she was watching all this from a distance. Even as she walked beside Katie Summer and kept careful time to the music, she didn't feel as if she was a part of what was happening.

Paige felt a touch against her arm and looked over at Katie Summer. Katie flashed her a quick, sly smile that brought a fleeting dimple to her cheek. Paige swallowed hard, ducked her head, and looked away. Later she would have to deal with this girl, but not now, not while her father was repeating the same vows he had made so many years before to her own mother.

But that quick glance had been enough to remind her of how wrong she had been about how Katie Summer would look in her matching pink dress. It made Paige feel leggy and graceless beside her.

All the Guthries were good-looking. Tucker was almost as tall as Paige's father, and comfortingly nice to look at in a different, curly-haired way. Mary Emily, behind with Megan, was button cute. But the girl at Paige's side was just too much! Katie's thick, dark blonde curls spilled in glorious profusion around her glowing face.

Her pink dress picked up the rosiness of her deep tan and showed off the sparkle of her laughing blue eyes. Paige held her head high, fighting a sudden feeling of inadequacy that made her breath come short.

Looking back, Paige was sure that the wedding brunch was as beautiful as any meal she would ever eat. As they ate, Grandma Summer bent to Paige to make conversation, her soft voice rising in an exciting, different rhythm. "Virginia Mae tells me you play the piano, Paige, and that you're an excellent student. My, I know your father is just *so* proud of you."

Before Paige could reply, Katie flipped her glowing head of curls, turned away, and put her hand on Paige's father's arm. "I just had a perfectly *terrifying* thought," she said, looking up into his face. "My goodness, I hope you don't expect *me* to have a lot of talents or be a bookworm. I've got to tell you right off that I don't believe in all that."

After an astonished look, Paige's father covered Katie's hand with his, and chuckled. "That's pretty interesting," he said. "What *do* you believe in, Katie Summer?"

Her laugh was quick and soft. "Having a *wonderful* time, just like I am today."

Naturally he beamed at her. Who could help it when everything she said sounded so intimate and appealing in that soft, coaxing drawl? Paige felt a shiver of icy jealousy. That Katie Summer was something else!